Carl Nixon is a full-time writer of short fiction and plays. His recent works for the stage include adaptations of Lloyd Jones' Deutz Medal winner *The Book of Fame* and J. M. Coetzee's Booker Prize winner *Disgrace*. The University of Canterbury has awarded Carl the 2006 Ursula Bethell Residency in Creative Writing, supported by Creative New Zealand. He lives in Christchurch with his young family.

fish'n'chip shop song

AND OTHER STORIES

carl nixon

VINTAGE

ARTS COUNCIL OF NEW ZEALAND *TOI AOTEAROA*

The assistance of Creative
New Zealand is gratefully
acknowledged by the author.

National Library of New Zealand Cataloguing-in-Publication Data
Nixon, Carl, 1967-
Fish 'n' chip shop song and other stories / by Carl Nixon.
ISBN-13: 978-1-86941-761-1
ISBN-10: 1-86941-761-5
I. Title.
NZ823.2—dc 22

A VINTAGE BOOK
published by
Random House New Zealand
18 Poland Road, Glenfield, Auckland, New Zealand
www.randomhouse.co.nz

First published 2006

ISBN-13: 978 1 86941 761 1
ISBN-10: 1 86941 761 5

Text design: Katy Yiakmis
Cover design: Matthew Trbuhovic
Cover images: Fish and chips — Photo New Zealand;
NZ infantry Faenz Italy (DA-07953-F) — Alexander
Turnbull Library, Wellington, New Zealand;
other photos — Matthew Trbuhovic
Printed in Australia by Griffin Press

For Rebecca

contents

king tut's last feather

When Maurice Harbidge was killed by a speeding sheep truck on a lonely bend of State Highway 73 it seemed only right that his best friend King Tut was with him. Eyes open, staring upwards, Maurice lay on a tussock-covered patch of ground. The spot was just past where the highway first scales the rugged defences of the Southern Alps and dips down again, flattening out near Lake Lyndon, frozen white in winter, and then winds along a broad valley at the foot of eroded mountain ranges. A great hollow in the mountains like vast cupped hands. A lonely place. The only sound after the initial squeal of brakes was the bleating of sheep from the decks of the truck that had killed him. Surrounded by the bald, shingle-topped mountains in this vastness of tussock land, King Tut stood beside Maurice's body and cried out his loss into the emptiness.

The young and the old are often the last to be told about

tragic events. Although I had seen him two or three times a week for my whole life, it wasn't until my mother sent me down to Mr Greenslade the butcher for a kilogram of lamb chops, to bring back wrapped in shiny greaseproof paper, that I heard the story of Maurice's death.

I was glad of the errand although I complained when asked to go, more out of a sense of twelve-year-old independence than real annoyance. The truth is that I was bored, and the short walk was a welcome diversion. The exhilarating freedom of December with the accompanying expectation of Christmas had been replaced by January apathy. My best friends Tim and Cam Marsden had gone away with their family to visit relatives in the North Island and wouldn't be back for days. School didn't start again for two weeks which was a lifetime.

I walked along the verge of the main road. Our town was built among the first pubescent swellings of the land into gentle foothills before the mountains. The smattering of shops and houses clung to the edge of the highway down which townies and tour buses and heavy trucks bound for the city or places north flashed by. People rarely slowed to the legal fifty kilometres an hour unless they were planning on pulling over to buy a milkshake from the dairy or a steaming packet of fish and chips from Mr Kimball's. People were eager to get to where they were going which was never here.

Parting the hanging strips of coloured plastic that kept the flies out, I went into the butcher's. Inside was goose-bump cool. The air drifted out from the open freezer in waves smelling of blood and seasoned sausage stuffing. Mr Greenslade glanced at me and raised his eyebrows in greeting but did not stop his conversation.

'I've got a cousin who's a traffic cop in Christchurch, so when I heard I rang him up after work and had a bit of a yarn.' The meat cleaver punctuated his words with the crunching crack of metal on bone.

'Is that right?' Willie Toogood's mother leaned forward. She wore a floral cotton dress and I noticed that the fat around her ankles spilled over the top of her shoes.

'Straight from the horse's mouth. In the Castle Hill Basin. They found the tyre-jack where he dropped it.' Thump. Bone being split from bone. 'He must've crouched down by the wheel and the sheep truck just came around a bit of a bend and clipped him.'

'How awful.'

I was only half listening. I stared blankly at a couple of fresh chickens naked and white in the window. Mr Greenslade's hands seemed to work by themselves as he quickly folded paper around the meat without looking down.

'The truck driver told the police that the poor bugger was lying in the tussock on the side of the road. Reckoned he looked like he was sleeping. Hardly a mark on him, although they're saying he must've died instantly.'

'How terrible.'

He handed the wrapped meat to Mrs Toogood and the till dinged as he rang up the sale. 'And that bloody parrot just sitting there on his chest.'

It was only then that I knew he was talking about Maurice. Maurice Harbidge who rolled my ice creams and scooped out the mixed lollies behind the counter of his mother's dairy. Tall, thin Maurice. Maurice with the high whistling laugh of a little boy. King Tut's friend and constant companion. Maurice was dead.

I was a country kid and thought that I knew about

death. I'd seen my father twist the necks of chickens with
a sudden violent wringing of his hands, and eaten them for
dinner just a few hours later. I'd shot rabbits for fun with
my cousin Mat's gun. But Maurice's death scared me.
Standing in the butcher's shop, it occurred to me that if
Death could round a bend smelling of sheep shit and hot
wool and take Maurice just like that, then He could come
for any one of us just as suddenly and in just as elaborate
a disguise.

I could not remember a time when the bird had not been
perched on Maurice's bony shoulder. King Tut gave
Maurice a certain piratical flair, a quality not often seen in
workers in the dairies of small rural towns. He was always
called King Tut. Never just Tut. As though King was a first
name like Matthew or Ben or Rangi. He was a large bird
with a powerful curved beak. 'A macaw,' Maurice called
him. 'All the way from South America.' And the colours.
King Tut shone red and orange and yellow and green and
at least three shades of blue near the tips of his wings. It
was hard to believe that such brightness existed in our
town. Colours that bright were reserved for the cars of rich
holidaymakers and skiers passing through, and for new
Coca-Cola billboards before dust from the passing trucks
turned them shades of grey.

    Six days a week you could find Maurice behind the
counter of his mother's dairy with King Tut sitting up on
his shoulder. My friends and I came in to buy white paper
bags stuffed with chewy milk bottles, Eskimo men in pink
and white, orange and chocolate jaffas or aniseed wheels,
bags of powdered sherbet. They all sat under the Harbidges'
glass counter, displayed like museum exhibits. Next to the

till was a jar full of liquorice straps curled up like garden snails.

At the sound of the bell over the door Maurice would appear from out the back where he lived with his mother, even though he was almost forty when he died. King Tut would bob up and down on Maurice's shoulder and twist his rainbow head from side to side in delight. Often he'd leap down and strut backwards and forwards along the counter.

'What can I do you for? What can I do you for?' Each word was a drawn-out croak like a rusty door hinge, but the meaning was always clear enough. King Tut had a whole heap of things he could say and just when you thought you'd heard them all Maurice would teach him a new one. 'Gidday, mate!' and 'Did ya like that then?' were two of his favourites. A few times I heard him sing the opening bars of Beethoven's Fifth. 'Dah dah dah dahhhh!'

'Good boy,' Maurice always said and rubbed King Tut on the top of his head.

'Good boy! Good boy!' King Tut would croak in delight.

Only a fool wouldn't have been able to tell that those two loved each other.

I'd heard Dad say once that Maurice 'wasn't the full quid' as if he was the same as Mr Winters who lived four doors down from us. On windy nights I would hear old Winters out in his backyard yelling dirty words at the sky and kicking the trunks of the pine trees, blaming them for his lack of sleep. He went on like that until his daughter came and took him inside. But Maurice wasn't at all the same.

Around his mother and other adults Maurice was

pretty quiet, but what most of them didn't know was that
Maurice was one of the most popular people in town. King
Tut made him a star. Kids went out of their way to come
into the shop just to see Maurice and King Tut. Walking
down the street, Maurice would be stopped every five
minutes by some kid wanting to talk about King Tut, how
he was and what new words Maurice had taught him.

But it was at the Saturday afternoon movies that
Maurice and King Tut achieved real fame. They attended
every week without fail, and sat in the same seats up the
front in the middle. It was a contest to see who would sit
next to Maurice and King Tut. Maurice never came with
anyone, not a girl or anyone, so the seats on either side
were always up for grabs. Kids arrived an hour early just
to get those seats. King Tut liked Westerns the best. He
would bob up and down faster and faster during the horse
chase scenes. Whenever there was a gunshot King Tut
would cry out, 'Take that ya varmint!' and Maurice would
open his mouth wide and laugh his high laugh along with
everyone else in the flickering light of the old movie
theatre.

It got to be a bit of a ritual that at the end of the movie,
when the good guy shot the baddy down in the street, all
the kids would yell along with King Tut.

'Take that ya varmint!'

King Tut would turn on Maurice's shoulder and face
the audience. He knew everyone was watching him and he
loved it. He'd bob up and down so that it looked exactly
like he was bowing. That bird was a born showman.

Although I was too young at the time to express it
clearly, I guess Maurice needed that bird. King Tut made
him whole. Without him Maurice would have just been

Mrs Harbidge's unmarried son who worked in the dairy six days a week. He might even have been a bit creepy, shy and tall and skinny as he was, the subject of kids' whispered conversations and shouted abuse. But with King Tut on his shoulder Maurice was the most popular guy in town.

The only person who didn't like King Tut was Maurice's mother. It was never anything she said that revealed her dislike. Not in front of the customers anyway. Her opinion of King Tut was revealed by small signs. Whenever the bird screeched or cried out, her pale forehead would corrugate up. Or her mouth would pucker into a tight bloodless hole — 'Her cat's ass mouth,' Tim called it — as she watched him pull affectionately at Maurice's ear.

Once I saw her putting tins of spaghetti on the shelves when King Tut screeched. In the background Mrs Harbidge simply froze, a tin of spaghetti suspended in the air, her neck stiff and white like plaster. No one else saw it. She stayed perfectly still and then she just moved again as if nothing had happened.

King Tut had been a present from Maurice's Dad just before he died of a heart attack. Looking back now, I don't think Mrs Harbidge ever forgave him either act.

I didn't go to the funeral. My mother said that a funeral was no place for a twelve-year-old. Instead I wandered down to the stand of gums near the church. The sap from the trunk stuck to my fingers and as I climbed I could hear the muted sound of a hymn. From the fork of a branch high above the ground I watched the people come out.

Mrs Harbidge wore an old-fashioned hat with a dark

veil that came down over her face. She stood alone near the hearse and people went up to her in ones and twos. Watching from the tree, it seemed they moved away quickly, afraid, I thought, to be near her too long in case her bad luck, like head lice, jumped over to them. And still I couldn't see King Tut. No flash of sunflower yellow or poppy red among the dark clothes of the mourners. There was no squawk or cry of 'Goodbye! Goodbye!' as the coffin was loaded into the long black hearse for the short drive to the cemetery.

'Of course Mrs Harbidge didn't bring the bird,' said my father when I asked him about it that evening. He seemed amused that I had mentioned it.

'I should think not,' said my mother. 'Imagine the squawking and carrying on.' She clanked the oven door shut to show that the topic was closed.

I didn't say anything, but it seemed to me that King Tut should have been the chief mourner. I imagined him sitting on top of the casket, his colours rivalling the stained-glass window behind. I didn't think he would have cried out or carried on during the service. After all, who loved Maurice more than King Tut?

I didn't see King Tut for just over a year after that.

At first the local kids talked about the accident and speculated about what had happened to King Tut. But as time slid by like a slow river they ceased to question where he was except perhaps as a passing thought brought on by a patch of deepest red in the sunset or a lime green wrapper blowing in the gutter.

I had only been back to Harbidges' Dairy once. Mrs Harbidge herself served me. She did not talk beyond telling me the price. Her face was as pale as the milk bottle sweets beneath the glass counter. I half expected King Tut to appear from the top of one of the shelves but there was no squawk or bobbing head. No flash of glowing feathers. The place was still and deserted. It was as though the bleakness of the high country where Maurice died had filled the shop. After that I bought my sweets at the new petrol station where everything was metal shelves and bright lights and I didn't have to think about Maurice.

But then it was autumn of the following year. I was alone and practising my place-kicking between the rugby posts down at the domain. The ball bounced end over end and over the fence into the back of Mrs Harbidge's section. As I bent down to pick it up from the unmown grass, I heard King Tut squawk.

My palm came away from the window black with dirt. Cupping my hand, I saw that a room at the back of the house had been turned into a dim store room full of junk and boxes. Mrs Harbidge had King Tut in the corner. He was in a rusted cage obviously made for a smaller bird, a canary or a budgie. At first I couldn't even tell if it was King Tut. His feathers were mostly gone, replaced by patches of wrinkled pale flesh. He reminded me of the baby rats Dad had found in a nest behind the wall and drowned. As I watched, King Tut squawked hollowly and shook the bars with his feet.

The window wasn't locked, and it rattled in its frame as I pried it up and climbed through. The room smelt of mildew and bird shit.

'Hey boy. Remember me?'

King Tut threw himself backwards, thrashing his wings. He squatted among the piles of white shit that had built up like stalagmites on the floor of the cage and glared at me with one yellowed eye. His plucked breast rose and fell. Watching him, I knew that King Tut was mad.

I imagined him there in the dark room every day since Maurice had died, shut in this cage with no one for company. I knew Mrs Harbidge would never talk to him, never take him out or stroke his head as Maurice had done. She'd obviously been giving him food and water, but that was it. I doubted King Tut had even seen a cage before this.

'It's going to be okay.' I poked my fingers through the bars, but he backed away. Shit streaked his remaining feathers. Reaching down, he yanked another feather from his breast. A thin trickle of blood followed the wrinkles of his pale skin. This was not the King Tut who sat on Maurice's shoulder bowing and playing to the movie crowd. Maurice's friend was gone, lost in endless days of loneliness and loss.

Slowly I opened the cage door. The hinges were stiff. King Tut backed away but hardly protested beyond a sad, distant muttering as I picked him up. His eyes rolled in his head. His heart was beating wildly against my palm and I saw that his feathers were faded. What future was there for King Tut now?

Twisting his head sharply in my hands, I heard a noise like a muffled twig breaking. I half expected a last defiant squawk, but King Tut made no sound.

King Tut's body lay in a white shoe box lined with tissue paper. The cemetery was on a gently sloping hill overlooking the road and the scattered houses, and was backed by a row of tall poplars. Their yellow leaves lay over the graves and in drifts against the headstones.

Using a trowel I had taken from my parents' garage, I buried King Tut in the grassy earth on top of Maurice's grave. To mark the spot I put a feather picked up from the floor under his cage. The end I planted in the ground so that it pointed upwards like a flag. I had washed it clean, and in the last sunlight that touched the hilltop the feather shone blue and green, brighter than anything this town had seen before. Or, in all likelihood, ever would again.

From the distant foothills a sheep's bleat drifted through the chill autumn air. As the last sunlight slipped beyond the mountains I imagined the cold emptiness of the high country slowly coming down and covering our town like a winter mist. Who was there to stop it now that Maurice and King Tut were gone?

The Apple of his Eye

His name was Coutts and he owned a fruit shop famous for its displays of highly polished produce. Every morning at first light Coutts emerged from his home above the shop and aligned the fruit on dimpled trays set on trestle-tables in the entranceway and outside on the swept footpath. He polished every item himself. People driving by on their way to and from work often felt compelled to pull over and admire the mirror-like sheen on a Granny Smith or gaze into the refulgent surfaces of the rows of Royal Galas. His persimmons were buffed the colour of the Australian outback. His oranges, mandarins and tangerines flared. His Splendours lived up to their name. Coutts did not stock kiwifruit, pears or pineapples — or any of the spiky, hairy or otherwise lacklustre fruits. And why should he? Admiring almost always led directly to buying. Business was booming.

Despite this loudness of trade, Coutts had two problems which occupied his mind. Firstly, he was unusually short, although it would be misleading for me to refer to him here as a dwarf. It would be an exaggeration for effect, a twisting of the facts. Or rather, a shrinking down, a compacting. He walked without the sea-swell roll of the true dwarf. His body was as lean as a nine-year-old's and his fingers would have easily allowed him to take up the piano should he have had the inclination. Which, for the record, he did not.

Being so short was, however, a distinct disadvantage in the day-to-day dealings of a fruiterer. To stock as much as was required, it was necessary to have numerous shelves both in the shop and out the back in the store room.

Shelves from the floor almost up to the ceiling.

An unnatural abundance of such shelves.

A very short man.

Do I have to spell it out further?

The second problem would take more than a ladder and stamina to overcome. Coutts had no children. He had been married, but his wife had left him in circumstances that were painful to recall. So painful that, although she was still alive, he thought of himself as a widower. While still together, they had tried to produce fruit from their loins. Upon gazing down a microscope, however, a doctor of the variety *specialist* had informed Coutts that his sperm were short in the tail. 'Poor swimmers, I'm afraid. Sorry.' Coutts's chances of bearing a child to inherit the fruit shop were as slim as a finger banana.

Even without a family, the life of a fruit-shop owner does not leave much time for leisure. True, Coutts liked to read in the evenings, biographies of shorter people mainly:

Napoleon was a favourite; Isaac Newton was only five foot one. But on the whole his long working days consisted of innumerable tasks pegged out beginning and end by the jumping jangle of the old-fashioned bell above the door. On Sundays, however, Coutts indulged himself. He would close the shop early and spend the last hours before dark wandering the docks and the hills behind the small port town where he lived. All the climbing up and down ladders had made him very fit, and being short is no impediment to walking.

Once upon one of these walks (a time, if you like details — 6.30) Coutts came across a woman. Her body was long and thin, more like an elongated vegetable — a runner bean perhaps — than a fruit. But her stomach bulged out in front of her as big as a watermelon. She was sitting on a porous stone wall that had been built to mark off the top of the old quarry. The woman's feet dangled and tears squeezed from the corners of her eyes. They dripped off the high curve of her cheeks on to the dusty stone, leaving small dark patches like seeds. When she leaned dangerously forward, one of the tears splashed on the rocks far below.

In case you feel the need to label this bulging bean, this ripe woman, I will tell you now that her name was Eyelash. Unusual, yes, but not unprecedented. After all, there are Rainbows and Skys and even Zowies out there to be met. The name Eyelash had been chosen by her mother after she misheard a conversation on a bus. A man sitting in front of her had referred in passing (in both senses) to the well-known actress, Eilish Moran. To the listening woman the name Eyelash seemed to belong with delicate things like lace and dandelions and powdered sherbet. Buses are loud. She was tired. She had not herself seen the diminutive actress on the footpath. It was an easy mistake to make.

But back to that wall above the quarry. Eyelash was so preoccupied with her crying and sighing and leaning forward that she did not notice Coutts's approach. As she pushed off with her hands, Coutts was able to lunge forward and grasp one blue-veined spindle of a wrist, the last part of her to try to vanish beneath the lip of the wall. Shortness does not exclude strength. Coutts was certainly strong enough to suspend the dangling wisp of a woman whose only claim to solidity was the bulge in her stomach.

You can be forgiven for your assumption that this is a love story, that Coutts and Eyelash were made for each other. It is not. They never were. In no way is this a story about the passion between a tall woman and a short man. In fact, once Coutts had dragged Eyelash back over the lip of the wall, they stood and studied each other and were mutually unimpressed. They were both panting, both somewhat shocked, both scraped red by the porous stone. Coutts observed that the woman he had saved had arms lined with very fine blonde hairs and that sometimes they covered freckles that reminded him of the blemishes on inferior fruit. The skin on her shoulder near the sway of her long dark hair was fashionably pale but seemed to absorb the light rather than to reflect it. For Eyelash's part, she had never been attracted to short men. She observed that the man who had interrupted her came only to halfway between her thrusting navel and the bottom of her slightly swollen and tender breasts. There was not, what those who reduce love to an exact science would call 'chemistry'.

It had taken Eyelash some time to conjure up the courage to jump. She was unsure if she would be able to perform the same magic trick again any time soon, and after the events of the last six months she was in the mood for talking. A lifetime behind a counter had shaped Coutts into an accomplished listener. They sat on either end of a bench placed there by the local council for its view of the roofs of the town and the bruise-blue sea beyond.

'He was the most gorgeous man I had ever seen,' began Eyelash.

'Ahhh, yes,' said Coutts, 'I suppose he was.'

She looked across to see if he was mocking her. His small but perfectly proportionate face was turned towards her in diligent concentration. She continued.

The story she told was original only in some of its minor details. The man Eyelash was in love with was a sailor. From Norway. Apparently his hair was especially blond and curly, his jaw chiselled. The sailor had climbed up a garden ladder to Eyelash's bedroom and sung her folk songs from his native country in muted tones so that her parents, asleep downstairs, did not hear. While still outside on the ladder, he had whispered to Eyelash that his name was Lars and that her eyes were more beautiful than the Aurora Borealis.

After several nights of such talk Eyelash had invited him in. It had been Lars who suggested that he sing to her beneath her duvet. Only to muffle the sound, you understand. For the sake of her sleeping parents. She had, perhaps naïvely, she now confessed, agreed. Once under the duvet one thing led to another. (Of course it did! thought Coutts, but he said nothing.)

On the day that Lars's ship had sailed for Sydney,

Eyelash discovered that she was pregnant.

'My father reacted very badly,' said Eyelash.

'Yes,' said Coutts, 'I suppose he did.'

'When I couldn't hide it any more, I told him. He yelled and screamed and threw all my clothes out of the house. My mother just watched. She didn't say a word.'

'If you don't mind me asking, how old are you?'

'I'm nineteen. In July.'

'Yes,' said Coutts, 'I suppose you will be.'

When all Eyelash's words had gushed out and even the final sighs had dripped away, they sat and regarded the town and the sea beyond. The sun was not quite down and there was no breeze. The air was as warm as a sun-ripened tomato.

At last Coutts put forward a suggestion. Eyelash could come and stay with him in the fruit shop. He stressed that she would have her own room — her own key was mentioned several times — and that the only tasks expected of her in return for her room and board would be some light work around the shop. Mainly retrieving things from high shelves, perhaps serving customers during the rush hour.

'Just until you patch things up with your parents or are able to make some other arrangement.'

Eyelash took to the fruit trade right away. The orderliness of the shelves, the rows of shiny fruit, appealed to her. Her long limbs were ideally suited to the tasks of reaching, stretching, grasping and shifting. The till caused her some trepidation but Coutts was a patient, methodical teacher. In no time, Eyelash was ringing up sales with relish.

Weeks passed like a river — in rushes and eddies.

Eyelash made several attempts to glue together her

shattered relationship with her parents. There was some softening from her mother. The father, however, remained as hard as a newly picked avocado. Even so, Eyelash was happy. She enjoyed living with Coutts. Despite his size, she found him pleasant company. She enjoyed her contact with the many satisfied customers. She even looked forward to polishing the fruit in the early hours, watching the sun rise while making something beautiful even more so.

Months passed like a smile in a crowd.

Eyelash had her baby and called him John. She knew what a blessing a plain, run-of-the-mill name would be in later life. The name's very plainness was her first gift to her son. Coutts also brought a gift to the maternity ward. A wooden apple made to order by a master carver from heart rimu. Coutts had oiled and polished it himself until it was the colour of flowing manuka honey.

Years passed like the echo of a laugh.

John grew up happily in the fruit shop. By the time he was six he was as tall as Coutts. At seven he was taller. He was, in relative terms, an easy child — quick to giggle, snort and laugh, slow to cry even after a hard fall. As far as appearances go, his hair was curly and dark, his body all ribs and long muscles, a hybrid, genetically stretched by an Aryan seafarer and a runner bean.

Coutts taught John all he knew about the fruit trade. How to display the fruit to draw in the customers like moths. Where to search for the blemished fruit the less scrupulous suppliers sometimes tried to hide on the bottom trays. The correct way to give change — counting up like the rungs of a ladder from the price. John was happy to learn. Even when he was much taller, he still looked up to Coutts.

There was a game that Coutts and John played when

there were no customers in the shop. One of them would hide the rimu apple. And, not unpredictably, the other would have to find it. In a fruit shop there are abundant nooks in which to hide a wooden apple. It was a game they had played even before John could walk. He would shuffle across the polished floor in the storeroom, looking behind boxes and inside the drifts of shredded packing-paper gathered in the corners. He gurgled and frothed happily as he hunted.

'I don't think you're ever going to find it,' Coutts would say in later games.

'I'll find it.'

'No, I don't think so. Not this time.'

'It's still *inside* the shop, isn't it?'

'Of course.'

'Am I getting warmer?'

'Now that would be telling, wouldn't it?'

John did always find it — eventually. And then it would be his turn to hide the apple for Coutts to find. Sometimes the game would take days. Once, when Coutts taped the apple to the top of the slowly turning wooden blade of the shop fan, it took John a whole week.

'That's not fair,' said John, coming down the ladder, shining apple in hand. 'You used tape.'

'All's fair in love and war,' said Coutts.

Nothing that seems perfect truly is. Or if, by some forgetfulness of Fate, it is, then it cannot stay that way for very long. Thirteen years was a good stretch.

One Tuesday (at 3.15 in the afternoon) Eyelash was standing by the polished spears of yellow bananas when the bell jumped and twitched. Coutts was out and she was in charge of the shop. She looked up and there was Lars.

He had come in looking for some fresh fruit after a long voyage. He wore a white jersey with a roll neck under a dark sailor's pea-coat. Lars took a few seconds to recognise Eyelash. (She forgave him instantly. It had, after all, been thirteen years.) The reunion was not as awkward as you might expect. They talked. He smiled and joked. Eyelash laughed. He reached out and held her hand. Eyelash blushed and was thrilled.

'John,' she said shortly afterwards, 'I would like you to meet your father.'

Lars took his new-found fatherhood in his stride. He embraced both the role and the boy. Lifting John off the ground, he spun him around. Several highly glazed passionfruit fell to the ground but no one noticed.

Lars had a proposition. He had held the position of captain for several years and had saved enough money to retire back to Norway. He had always planned that this would be his last voyage. Why didn't Eyelash and John come with him? They would buy a small house on the edge of a wood and live happily. Eyelash thought about it. Several seconds later she agreed.

For his part John was delighted to find his real father. He asked if the house would be made of logs.

'If you want. Whatever you want.'

To cut a short story even shorter, that night Eyelash told Coutts that she and John were leaving. They packed their bags.

'I'll be sorry to see you go,' said Coutts. He thought that she was making a mistake but did not say anything. That night he did not sleep.

And then it was the next morning. There was a low cloud and a thin drizzle. The wooden planks of the wharf were stained black. There were tears as John and Eyelash hugged him and then walked up the gangway to where Lars was waiting. Coutts watched as the thick rope was set free and the ship edged away. He stood and waved for a long time, and then walked up the road to the place above the quarry where he could watch the ship move slowly out to sea. The wind was colder than he remembered it.

I would like to say that they all lived happily ever after.

Lars and Eyelash were married in a very traditional way but the house they bought was not by a wood. In fact, it was less of a house and much more of an apartment in the city. It was not, of course, made of logs. Years of being a ship's captain had made Lars quick to criticise. He was a man who felt he had a right to order others or to comment on the neglected corner of a newly mopped floor or the slightly burnt base of an anniversary cake. Other seafaring habits also remained. Married life had shrunk a woman in every port down to a woman in every road in the seedier district of the city.

During the interminably long, dark days of the Scandinavian winter, Eyelash found comfort in her adopted country's soft, satisfying pastries. In a few years her thin frame was draped with fat. She became a pumpkin of a woman. Thus insulated, she started a day-care centre for young unmarried mothers in an empty apartment in her building. She had developed into a good listener from working in the fruit shop, and no matter how many times she heard the same story she always made it seem as though it were the first.

'Yes,' she always said, 'I suppose he was.'

Eyelash was not unhappy in her new garb, in her new life. Nor was she completely happy. Sometimes she missed her old life in the fruit shop in the small town by the sea. Such is life.

As for John, he adapted well to his new homeland. Despite the peculiarity of the locals' pronunciation of his name, he went on to do well at school and eventually to study business at the city's university. After graduating he opened a vegan restaurant. It was so successful that one restaurant quickly grew into a string, spanning continental borders and, later, whole continents. Despite his success, John still ordered all the fruit and vegetables himself. I believe he still calls the small man he thinks of as his father regularly and they discuss the ups and downs of the produce business.

In the fruit shop, in a street, in a small town on the other side of the world, Coutts still serves behind the counter. To his customers he seems happy enough. He's always ready to talk about the weather, although his hair has greyed and he no longer gets up and down the ladder the way he once did. He can still be seen polishing fruit outside the shop in the early hours of the morning. But if you go and stand outside on a Sunday evening, after he has closed early, you can look through the slightly frosted glass of the door. You will probably see him playing a game. As you watch, he will carefully hide a piece of wooden fruit.

'I don't think you're ever going to find it,' he says to himself. 'Not this time.'

The Battle of Crete

It is Margaret who, against character, persuades Ron to return to Crete. Normally his daughter dissuades him from doing anything at all adventurous. Ron has been made to solemnly promise that he will no longer climb the ladder to clean out his own spouting. Navigating the uneven bricks in his garden path is, apparently, a shattered hip in the making. He has been ordered to forego the primitive joy of burning off his rubbish in the rusty half-drum at the bottom of the garden in case he loses his balance and it becomes a funeral pyre. In company Margaret will not hear a word said against her father. She tells people that Ron is remarkable for his age. She praises his tenacious independence and extols the virtues of the elderly living in their own homes for as long as is practical. But when they are alone together his daughter makes it clear she believes him to be standing on the brink of the slipperiest of slopes.

Which is why he is surprised by her reaction when he tells her about the letter from the president of the Crete Veterans' Association. They are sitting in the crowded food court of East Gate Mall. Margaret brings him here at least once a month. They stock up on necessary supplies at Pack 'n' Save and then afterwards she insists on buying him lunch. He always orders what used to be called a toasted sandwich but now has a flash Italian name. There are potted olive trees in a row along the edge of the tables.

'Next May,' he explains, just making conversation, 'is the sixtieth anniversary. There is a contingent of veterans going and I've been invited to join them.' He adds, 'Daft buggers,' to show that he is not considering going.

Margaret is suddenly animated. She is eating sushi, dipping a roll in a small plastic tub of soy sauce. She gestures in a broad arch with her chopsticks. 'But you must go. It's important.' Her movements are inappropriately large for the food court where the crowded tables force people to sit closer than is comfortable and where most tuck their shoulders forward as if protecting their plates from looters. Other diners glance nervously across at her.

'Why is it important?' he asks, surprised.

'Because this will be your last chance to go back, to revisit where it all happened.'

He does not know what Margaret imagines happened to him on Crete. Over the years he rarely spoke of the war to his wife and three children, and then only in the most general of terms. Any image his daughter has of his role in the Battle of Crete has not been lifted from his memories. But he does not deny that this will be his last chance. Although he will not confess it to Margaret, he is aware that his body might even now not be up to such a trip.

Lately he has been feeling nauseous most of the time and losing weight, and there has been blood in his faeces, which has scared him, though he has not yet sought treatment. He will hold out as long as he can before seeing a doctor. He knows that a diagnosis, once uttered, is as impossible to take back as a husband's slap. A doorway to a room he is not yet prepared to enter.

Ron is seventy-nine and hopes that he will not see eighty-five. A sudden sniping heart attack is his preferred cause of death — a shot out of the blue. Certainly, on his present downward trajectory, he cannot imagine anything beyond eighty-five that would be worth waiting around for. He tells Margaret that he will consider the trip, but upon being dropped home he slips the letter into the cluttered bottom drawer of his desk and, with the ease of a lifetime's practice, puts any thoughts of Crete out of his mind.

Margaret, however, is a determined woman. For many years she steadfastly managed a company importing athletic shoes from Japan. Even though she is now almost sixty and has taken early retirement, she habitually wears the brand out of corporate allegiance. Once set upon a course she rumbles steadily forward. She rings her father the next afternoon. She has been in contact with Alan Harbidge from the RSA. Apparently they had a very long and fruitful conversation.

'Is that right?' Ron is standing in the hall holding a fried bacon sandwich. The bread is still warm and greasy with oil. But he is feeling nauseous again, his stomach like a scrunched bag. He places the plate on the hall table, the sandwich barely touched.

'Yes. We sorted out a lot.'

Ron stands in his hallway and listens to Margaret itemise departure dates and travel itineraries. The airforce is apparently putting on a Boeing to fly the veterans to Greece.

'The prime minister is going,' she tells him. 'She will take part in the official ceremony.' As if pulling a rabbit from a hat, Margaret finally informs him of how much the entire trip will cost. 'Give or take about five hundred dollars.'

'It's not a question of money.'

'Of course it isn't.'

'I'm not sure that I want to go.'

'I understand. But I truly believe you'll enjoy it when you're there, and of course Peter and I will be along to look after you.'

'Look, there's someone at the door. I'll call you back later eh.'

He hangs up the phone and stands to finish his sandwich. There is no one at the door. The lie has gained him a few yards of safe ground. He wipes his fingers on the back of his trousers and goes out through the sun room on to the back lawn. The first autumn leaves sit on the lawn under the maple tree curved upwards like miniature boats, barely touching the grass. He sits in the sun on the wooden bench he made himself.

So. Margaret wants him to go back to Crete and she intends to come with him. Up until now he had imagined her plan involved sorting out itineraries, passports and travellers' cheques and then driving him to the airport, waving goodbye at the departure gate. But no. She is going to hold his hand. And she wants to bring Peter. Peter, her husband, is a respected landscape artist, established in his field: darkly atmospheric oils of New Zealand bush and mountains. Ron has a lot of respect for his son-in-law's work but does not have any store of warmth for the man himself. Peter, a lapsed Bohemian, still with a beard, seems at his best when actively painting. In the hours when he is not practising his art, the man has an air of irritability. He is tall and thin and strides round the house like a giraffe with toothache.

It is Ron's belief that as an artist Peter is too used to shaping his own reality. He is always the first to find fault with the details and inconveniences of day-to-day living. Nor have the high prices that his paintings now fetch brought Peter any obvious peace of mind. Ron is glad that he himself had no artistic urges. He had earned a living first as a builder and in later years a building inspector with the council. Both jobs were demanding in their own way, satisfying, but did not take you over. Something like painting could do that, he knew. In the army Ron had done basic training with a writer in the next bunk. A little bloke not much over five foot who everyone called Lofty. Even when they were exhausted from marching all day you could hear him in the dark, scribbling away under his blanket by the light of a torch. There is, Ron reflects now, a very thin line between Muse and Harpy. All things considered, he wishes his daughter had married someone with less of a calling.

Ron suspects Peter of having an affair. Just over six months ago, through the condensation-covered window of a crowded winter bus, he glimpsed Peter in a café in a posture of intimacy with another woman. He said nothing about it to Margaret at the time. He could have been mistaken in his interpretation of the fleeting tableau. It was hard to see properly. The window of the bus was running with water so that the world outside looked almost aquatic. He was past in a flash. With no further evidence, Ron was unwilling to toss suspicion across his daughter's marriage like poisoned confetti on the steps of the church.

Over the following weeks Margaret's conversation turns like an only half-felt change in the weather from probabilities to certainties and then swings around in a sudden gust in the direction of definite plans. His own explicit consent for the trip does not seem to be required. The truth is that he is ambivalent. On one hand it is an adventure, almost certainly his last. On the other he is reluctant to stir up old memories that he has been happy living without. Still, Ron never puts his foot down. He never comes out and says to Margaret's face that he does not want to go back to Crete; that he will not under any circumstances be conscripted into his daughter's mini echelon. And so equivocation is the means whereby he finds himself assisted aboard an Airforce Boeing by a young soldier in dress uniform who grips his elbow too hard.

The plane is full of old men in new suits. They sit scattered throughout the mostly empty seats, rustling through bags, whispering. There are thirty-three veterans all up. Most of them are accompanied by their daughters, although there are sons and even a few grandchildren. Everyone seems excited and nervous in equal parts.

It is a long flight. They stop at Perth and then in some Middle Eastern country where no one disembarks. Two men come on board and check everyone's passports. They are very friendly, all white teeth and expensive linen suits. But behind them two soldiers in pale blue uniforms stand by the door with machine-guns casually hanging from shoulder straps. Ron can suddenly feel the weight of his own rifle, the way the strap pulled down across the top of his neck during the long night march through the mountains of Crete. He excuses himself and goes to the tiny bathroom where he splashes water on his face and stays for longer than he needs to. When he returns the soldiers have gone and it is almost time to take off again.

'I was getting worried,' says Margaret.

He grunts. 'Sometimes things take a bit longer than they used to.'

The official doctor talks to Ron several times during the flight. Ron watches him move down the plane from old man to old man like an insect buzzing from ear to ear. The man is too loud and too jovial. He twice reminds Ron to keep his fluids up. When he approaches again they are over the Mediterranean and making their descent into Athens. Ron pretends to be asleep. There is a whispered conversation with Margaret. Her father, she says, is doing fine, considering.

They spend half a day and a night in Athens. Ron hates the place and wants to stay in his hotel room.

'I saw enough from the bus coming in.'

'Don't be silly. You didn't come halfway around the world to see the inside of a hotel room.'

'Why not? It's a very nice hotel room.'

But Margaret insists that they at least visit the Acropolis and perhaps an outdoor market, and he reluctantly agrees. Peter declines to join them. Apparently he has business at the New Zealand Embassy. At the end of the taxi ride to the Acropolis the driver tries to charge them ten times the standard fare, something Margaret has researched in advance. They are double parked in a narrow road, and while his daughter haggles in cold tones, Ron looks out the window. There are tourists everywhere. They jostle past, heading towards the beginning of the road up to the ruins like a school of impatient fish heading in to the mouth of a net. The skyline is a tangle of TV aerials and power lines. The buildings are concrete, square and ugly, and the sky is the white of bleached bones. While he watches he can feel the heat seeping through the glass of the window. The taxi's air-conditioning struggles noisily to keep it at bay. He moves back from the window and has a sudden hot twisting pain in his stomach. He hears himself let out a gasping grunt which he manages to half-swallow. He draws his knees up against the pain.

'I need to go back to the hotel,' he says quietly.

Both Margaret and the driver are so caught up in their negotiations that they do not hear him.

'Margaret!'

They both stop and turn, surprised.

'I'm not feeling well. I need to go back to the hotel.'

'What is it?'

'It's nothing. Probably just something I ate.' He forces himself to smile. 'But I need to lie down.'

Back at the hotel, the pain gets worse but he does not tell Margaret. He does not want that fool of a doctor examining him, asking questions to which he will have to lie. Instead he goes to his room, insisting on walking unaided. He takes several strong painkillers he has hidden in his suitcase and lies down on the bed. Certain positions, he discovers, make the pain subside for a while. Margaret pokes her head in after half an hour and Ron pretends to be asleep so she leaves quietly. Eventually he does sleep.

But he dreams of being shot in the stomach and being left behind by his mates in a steep, rocky ravine from which he knows there is no escape.

The next morning he feels fine. The pain in his stomach is gone, and he eats a good breakfast of yoghurt and honey and even manages a piece of toast. Then they are bused back to the airport. As they are being herded into the plane again one of the old-timers ahead of him bleats like a sheep. It is a very accurate imitation and a ripple of laughter moves through the crowd. Ron smiles.

Less than an hour later he is, after sixty years almost to the day, back on Crete.

Hania is an immediate disappointment to him. He does not know what he was expecting. But not this. Some of the pastel-coloured Venetian buildings still remain or have been reconstructed, he is unsure which. But it is the atmosphere that he finds hardest to reconcile with his memories. There is a commercial bustle, an air of modernity and noisy transience. Tourist buses park two deep on one side of Planteia 1866, the main square. There are neon signs. Family groupings of pale English and Americans march two abreast on the narrow streets, parents followed by children, clutching souvenirs and craning forward to see anything that might be in the least historical. He finds it all hard to reconcile with his patchy memories of curfewed streets and determined men hurrying past in drab uniforms.

There are three days before the official ceremony.

'Time to look around,' says Margaret on the morning of the following day. 'To get reacquainted.'

'Is Peter coming with us?'

'No.'

Since their journey began at Auckland Airport, Peter and Margaret have hardly spoken and then only in brief skirmishes, aiming to wound. Ron is a neutral observer to these exchanges. Throughout the flight to Crete Peter had sat apart. He read books on the island, often pausing to scribble in a blue notebook. Margaret has told him that Peter has been given some type of government funding. A grant, apparently, for a series of commemorative paintings which are to hang in the section of the Auckland Museum dedicated to the wars.

Peter left their pension early on the first day in Hania and has not reappeared, and Ron assumes he is on some type of official business.

Margaret and Ron travel on foot, resting often in shop doorways where Margaret browses until she sees that he is ready to go on. They sit on the benches under shade trees and watch people pass. Ron finds himself tiring easily and his daughter is content to blame it on the heat. Without planning their route they make their way naturally down to the water and sit outside a café at a table under a tall elm tree. There is a slight breeze coming off the harbour. They have a view of the water and the old stone wall which circles the harbour and of the small colourful fishing boats nearby. They have ordered bottled water which they sip out of ice-cold glasses.

'Shall we have some lunch?' Margaret asks suddenly.

'Why not eh.' He has lost track of time. He guesses that it is three or even four o'clock and he has not eaten anything all day except a small sweet pastry at breakfast, but the truth is he is not hungry. His stomach feels small and bitter and hard like an apricot from which the sun has sucked all the moisture. Margaret has a salad of olives and bright-red tomatoes and a fillet of soft marinated fish served cold. To keep up appearances and not worry her, Ron orders a chicken breast. But it is stuffed with strong-smelling goat's cheese and he can eat only a small fraction before admitting defeat. He sees her watching him and forces another mouthful.

'Don't you like it?'

'No, it's good.'

'You've hardly touched it.'

'I guess I'm just a bit jet-lagged. My stomach doesn't know if this is breakfast or a midnight feast.' She smiles with him and relaxes, but Ron knows that he will not be able to fool her for much longer, not Margaret.

When he finally gets back to his room, it is evening and he is totally drained. The room looks out over a rear courtyard where bags of refuse are temporarily stored. The smell of decaying food soaks the air outside, forcing him to keep his window closed. There is a knock on his door.

'Don't worry. It's just me.'

Margaret comes in and sits on the edge of his bed. She wants to know his response to being back on Crete. The truth is that Ron feels as if he has come to somewhere entirely new. The only sights which have stirred his memory are the Mediterranean itself, laid out at the foot of the town like blue-glazed ceramic, and the occasional glimpse of old women dressed from head to toe in black. There is little sense of return. He knows he could, if he wanted to, uncover buried memories, unearth his mates' faces and moments of laughter or pants-shitting fear. But what would be the point?

'It's certainly interesting,' is all he says.

Margaret seizes upon this crumb, smiles and nods.

'Yes. It is.' She starts to talk about small things they have seen that day and the arrangements for the ceremony down at the old landing field over which the PM will preside. He watches Margaret's hands as she speaks. She is biting her nails again, a habit she gave up when she was much younger but has recently resumed. He contemplates the vertical wrinkles at the top of his daughter's upper lip and reflects that surely it is unnatural for parents to live long enough to see their children move through middle age into the gaunt, infertile landscape beyond. People could be forgiven for mistaking them for an older brother and sister.

After Margaret leaves him he dozes but is woken in the darkness by Peter's footsteps on the marble staircase. Ron lies in his bed, staring up at the white ceiling, grey in the near darkness, and the silhouette of the slowly turning overhead fan. The only light comes in from the streetlights and is filtered through the wooden shutters. Margaret and Peter are in the next room and the thick plaster wall only muffles their sibilant fighting. As he listens Ron remembers the way that Peter leaned towards the woman in the coffee shop — arm extended, hand draped lightly over her upturned wrist as though caught in the act of checking her pulse. He wonders how much longer his daughter's marriage can hold out, who will be worn down into submission first? If it is Peter who leaves Margaret, then there is almost undoubtedly another woman. He knows from experience that, once dug in, men seldom fall back without first preparing another position. He lies awake in the darkness and listens long after the fighting has stopped: dogs barking; drunken shouts in English that quickly pass; and much later the noise of the tour buses coughing awake like chronic smokers before the first cigarette of the day.

It has been prearranged that the next morning all three of them will drive inland along the route that the retreating Allies took to the evacuation point at Sphakia. Peter wants to takes some photographs and to draw some preliminary sketches. He drives a rented Fiat quickly down the narrow roads. He hunches behind the wheel and scratches nervously at his beard when unsure of which way to turn. Next to him Margaret half turns her body towards the window. Ron is relegated to the back. As if, he reflects, he is a child or the family dog. From there he observes that the temperature in the car is far below that which the primitive air-conditioning could ever hope to provide.

They travel through several small villages, white-washed groups of houses on dusty patches of land. Old men sit outside in twos and threes and stare unblinking into the car as they pass. The landscape is uninspiring, rocky gullies with hills planted in rows and rows of low olives and the barren slopes of the steep mountains further inland.

'Ron. This is the road to Sphakia. Does anything look familiar?' Peter looks hopefully back at him in the rear-view mirror.

Ron looks around and sees a sealed road with smoothed out edges where the mountain has been bulldozed and dynamited away. His memory semaphores him images: the rocky trail over the mountains; Barry Bunker's tanned face laughing in the torchlight; sleeping under an olive tree only feet from the corpse of a young German still tangled in his parachute; the heels of the bloke in front who later drowned.

'No,' he says to Peter. 'We marched at night to avoid being bombed and strafed from the air.'

'But nothing looks familiar?'

He considers. 'Yes, one thing does.'

Peter looks expectantly back at him.

'There were olive trees.'

Peter frowns and does not ask Ron any more questions.

They have just left a village and the narrow road has flattened out, falling away on one side into a dry stream bed, when Ron hears a sudden intake of breath from Margaret. There is a solid thump as something hits the front of the car, and then Peter is braking hard.

'Did we hit someone?' asks Ron, alarmed.

'A dog,' says Peter. 'No, it was just a dog.'

Margaret is the first out of the car. When Ron reaches her she is kneeling next to the dog's body and lifting its head so it rests on her wrist like a pillow. The animal is clearly dead, sprawled half in the narrow ditch which runs along the downhill side of the road. Margaret's white cross-trainers look bright against the brown earth. It is a small dog and almost the same colour as the ground, as if it has evolved to be camouflaged in this landscape. Its legs are too short for its body and its fur is mangy. A mongrel and probably a stray. The only sign of the car's impact is a small smear of blood on the ground beneath the dog's flank. Flies are already starting to gather. Margaret is holding the dog, stroking along its neck.

'It's dead,' says Peter. 'We should go.' He stands behind them close to the car, and looks around as though expecting angry Cretans to emerge from among the olive groves demanding remuneration or revenge.

Margaret is still crouching, stroking the dog's head. 'You were driving too fast.'

'It darted out.'

'If you'd been going slower you could have missed it.'

'What does it matter? It's just a stray bloody dog.'

Margaret lays the dog's head down carefully. She straightens and stares at Peter coldly and then walks back to the car. Peter follows her without looking at the dead dog. He slips his long body behind the wheel and slams the door. Ron is the last to climb back in.

They drive on into the mountains with only the noise of the straining motor in the small space. After another hour the car pulls off the road which has been climbing steadily. They have come to the broad saddle of the road before it dips down again. Peter announces into the sudden silence that he is going to go on foot to a point where he can look down and sketch the Askifou valley, parts of which they can glimpse ahead. 'In their journals several New Zealand soldiers commented on being inspired by the sight of the valley among the mountains.' He looks at Ron for confirmation but Ron looks away back towards Hania and the sea and says nothing. Peter sighs. He takes his bag with his camera and pencils and sketch pad, and walks towards a stand of pine trees up the hill.

'Wait.'

Margaret gets out and follows him. Ron stays in the car. Although he cannot hear clearly what is said, Ron watches as Margaret begins to berate Peter bitterly, at first about the dog but then about other things. The name Carolyn is mentioned several times. For once Peter does not defend himself. He stands, tall and thin on the side of the dusty road, and faces Margaret as she expels her anger into his face. Embarrassed for them both and for himself, Ron looks away.

When Margaret finally returns to the car, her face is

tight. Peter has gone, vanished across the road and into the trees. Without a word she collects a basket from the boot and takes Ron by the arm, leading him over a ditch and into the olive trees growing up the side of a small hill. Ron is soon breathing heavily so that Margaret stops walking and spreads out a blanket on an almost level patch of ground beneath a tree.

'Here. Sit down.'

He sits carefully, feeling his knees twinge. From the basket, Margaret takes crusty bread and cheese bought in Hania that morning. There is bottled water and red wine. The leaves cast dappled shadows that move slightly around them as she lays out the food. The trunk of the olive tree behind them is forked with age and the wood twists in on itself like the thick plaited bread Ron suddenly recalls the islanders baking for weddings. For the first time in a long while he feels hungry and is grateful.

As she lays out the food on the blanket Margaret begins to cry. She turns away, hiding her face so that he will not notice. He cannot remember seeing his daughter cry since she was a very small girl. Still sitting, he reaches out and pulls her close to him so that her head is against his chest. At first she resists, but then he feels her surrender. She starts to sob and he soothes her, making small cooing noises as he remembers he used to do when she was young and would wake in the night. He sees that there is a small patch of maroon blood from the dead dog dried on the edge of her sleeve. He does not know how long he stays that way, holding her. Until the shadows have moved, growing longer and swinging further to the east.

When he is sure that Margaret is asleep Ron lowers her gently so that she is lying on her side on the rug, her face away from the sun, and then he stands using the trunk of the olive tree for support. He picks up a piece of bread and some cheese. Remarkably he is still hungry. In fact he is ravenous. He walks a short distance and stands eating, ripping the crusty bread with his hands and laying the cheese inside in thick wedges. The land falls away from the spot where he has stopped. In the distance is the blue of the Mediterranean. He can see the rows of olive trees and the road to Sphakia winding up through the mountains, hugging the edge of a ravine, and their car parked on the side of the road. There is no sign of Peter.

As he eats his bread and cheese he stands with one hand against a rough trunk and feels the wind off the sea on his face. He eats as slowly as possible, savouring the taste and the place. There are no exhilarating flashbacks to falling paratroopers or German bombers swinging in along the road. Small personal things have stayed with him from his days on Crete, but the war was sixty years ago and he has other stronger memories from his life. Better memories to make a raft of now. In this moment there is only the peppery taste of good strong cheese. There is only his knees aching from the climb, blood in his stool and his sleeping daughter who is almost an old woman herself and whose marriage is probably over.

The seduction

ere's to Shakespeare!'
 'To Willy!'
 The final curtain call had been several hours ago, and the last of the amateur dramaturgs had given up trying to catch the director's eye and drifted away into the night. Now only the remnants of the cast and crew were left, clustered in small groups around the foyer. As they drank they consumed the remaining free food in the manner of underpaid contract workers unsure of their next job. A few tepid and flaking sausage rolls, squares of yellow cheddar on toothpicks and a runtish lamington were all that were left from the opening-night spread put on by the ladies of the Royal Theatre Supporters' League.

'To the best show this side of Sydney!'

'*Titus*!'

'*Tight Ass*!' Alastair Howard raised his wine glass.

The other actors moved their bodies closer and roared

with laughter at this running gag.

Over at her table Karen smiled, in on the joke. The actors' laughter was projected around the small space, bouncing off the fake Doric columns. Well-modulated tones echoed back from the mouths of the figures in the old production photographs hanging around the walls. Karen sat at her table with the other backstage crew but often looked towards the bar where the actors gathered like bright birds. The company at Karen's own table were more subdued. Half a dozen backstage crew dressed in black discussed problems of lighting, sound and costuming with untrained voices while empty bottles of Steinlager and DB collected in front of them. Karen crushed out her cigarette in an ashtray shaped like the two Greek masks, Comedy and Tragedy. It was Comedy who had the ash ground into his metal eye.

'The butt of my joke,' she said, and laughed out loud.

There were nervous smiles. When she tried to explain, the others just stared and smiled harder.

'I get it,' said Michael from set construction. He leaned towards her with a lopsided smirk. Karen noticed that he had not been able to completely remove the green paint from his fingernails. His aftershave was inadequate to hide the occasional heady waft of turps. They had once fumbled together backstage during a performance of *Suddenly, Last Summer*. It was a move that she had instantly regretted. She blamed the lapse on the turps fumes radiating from his body which had made her giddy and easily susceptible to his advances.

Another burst of laughter came from the direction of the bar, and the actress talking to Alastair flicked her blonde hair away from her face with the back of her pale hand.

As more and more people drifted away, Karen stood and walked, only slightly unsteadily, towards the toilets. She stopped for a moment in front of the photograph wall. Years ago the wall had displayed portraits only of the actors who were full members of the Royal company (and back then, strictly paid-up members of Actors' Equity too). Now, in more egalitarian times, the technicians, stage managers and other backstage crew had been allowed their 8 by 10 square of fame.

Karen's own face was displayed in the first row, second from the end. In the alphabetical hierarchy, Burrows placed her near the top, between the general manager's secretary and an older actor named Chamberlain who couldn't manage accents apart from his own (which a barb doing the rounds said he could only just manage), plus southern American and bog Irish. He wasn't in *Titus*, which the director had set in colonial New Zealand during the land wars and therefore required a selection of English and Maori vowels. With a professional's eye, she saw that the photographer's lighting was too stark to flatter her pink-toned skin and that the slightly upwardly angled illumination created the vague impression that her eyes were about to pop from her head. But it was not lighting that made her face so broad, as if she were a Russian peasant in a play by Chekhov. Lighting could not mask her naturally thick neck nor her broad long-distance-swimmer's shoulders. Like the tip of an iceberg, they hinted at the big bones, the wide expanse of bosom and rolling hips beneath.

Even as Karen gazed at his face, Alastair Howard's hand came down, oh so gently, on her shoulder. 'Just checking out the wall of fame?' he asked. His eyes lingered on his image but his hand stayed on Karen's shoulder. His palm felt hot against her skin even through the cotton of her dress. Alastair was tall, over six foot, with the slightly deflated look of a naturally large man who has achieved slimness through a strict and almost exclusive diet of strong black coffee and Marlboro Lights. His hair was just beginning to turn grey above the ears. Either that, she thought, or he was dying it grey to look more sophisticated.

'I just wanted to say that I love what you've done with the lighting on this show. Fantastic. It really is fantastic.' His voice was a rumbling base. His eyes were aqua-blue and she wondered about the rumours that he wore tinted contact lenses. Karen imagined that she saw him glance down at her breasts which were an expanse of only slightly mottled skin above the low scoop of her purple dress. She felt herself begin to breathe faster.

'Thanks. I'm pretty happy with it.'

'And so you should be. It's fantastic. Really.'

There was a pause in which Karen knew she should say something but couldn't think what. Instead she studied the photographs intently, in a way that she hoped made her appear studious and intelligent. A woman who had mastered her field. Who was ready to seize any opportunities life might toss her way.

'Karen, the thing is, and I know it's terrible of me to ask, but I'm in a spot of trouble and I was wondering if you could help me out. There's been a bit of unpleasantness with one of my flatmates. She's moving out but I'd rather not go back there tonight. If you know what I mean.' He smiled as broadly as his photograph.

'Yes.'

'The point is, I need a place to stay for the night and

Tim said that your flat is near here?'

She nodded.

'Please say no if it's a hassle. Really.'

Karen had a sudden image of Alastair Howard slipping off his shiny blue shirt and letting it fall on to the floor of her bedroom. She could almost feel him run the tips of his long fingers over her lips.

'It's not a problem.'

'Are you sure? You're not just saying that?'

'No, really.'

'Excellent. You're a wonder. I can't tell you what this means to me.' He hugged her tightly and she felt the warmth of his breath on her neck and the firm push of his chest against her breasts. 'I've got a photo-call in the morning so I hope you don't mind if we leave pretty soon?'

'No. Sure. I was going to leave anyway.'

'Excellent. I'll get my coat.' He flashed her his best smile as he went to say his goodbyes.

He kept her waiting for only twenty minutes but by that time the rain had started to fall in a soft mist. 'Shit.' Alastair pulled his collar up around his ears. Karen thought it was remarkable how much he looked like James Dean in that photograph taken on the bridge, and wondered if he knew.

There were a few people standing under the eaves.

'See you all anon,' said Alastair. 'Great show everyone.'

An actor with only a minor role held out a joint and Alastair paused long enough to take a drag. He offered some to Karen and she took a shallow puff, feeling the dampness of his mouth against her lips.

'Party's just gearing up. Hang around for a bit,' the actor said.

'I've got to go. I need my beauty sleep.' Alastair winked

and of course people laughed, and then he was moving away with Karen behind him like a shadow. There was a burst of laughter as someone said something not meant for Karen to hear.

They crossed the road and then hurried from the overhang of one tree to another. It was cold and the southerly wind forced its way into the light coat she had pulled on over her dress. Suddenly it began to rain harder. Their only warning was the rising hum of rain hitting the road and bouncing off the roofs of the nearby buildings. A downpour with raindrops that jumped up at them from the tar-seal.

'In here,' said Alastair. He led the way into the doorway of a bar to wait it out.

'Where's this Aladdin's Cave of yours then?' His chocolate voice was raised over the sound of the rain.

'It's just over on Winton Street, not far, but it's not much really.' Karen ran her hand over her sodden hair.

'Any port in a storm.'

Karen laughed too hard. A couple pushed past them and went into the bar, shaking the water off their coats. Music, throbbing and vibrant, washed over them. She hoped that Alastair would invite her inside for a drink. Just the two of them. Maybe they would dance. But he said nothing, just stared mysteriously out at the rain. She gazed up at his rugged profile and wondered what to say to break the ice.

'You must miss Alex,' said Karen at last.

Alastair blinked twice. He seemed for a moment not to know to whom she was referring. 'Um, yes, I do. But the part in *Shortland Street* was fantastic. It's not like she could turn it down.'

'I guess.'

Karen thought of Alex with her boy's hips and aggressive pout and her competitive aversion to other women. She also remembered Tania who Alastair had been seeing during *The Crucible*. And Chantel whose real name was Shiree. Alastair had been seeing her for a while too, but they'd broken up during the final night of *The Wind in the Willows*. Chantel/Shiree had raged, screaming and swearing in the rehearsal room and throwing props, while most of the cast and crew pushed and shushed and giggled in the narrow hallway outside the door. It was a performance that everyone agreed was better than her somewhat stilted Mole. And Tarra. She'd been the one Alastair left his second wife for. They'd been caught in the costume room by the night cleaner, Alastair leaning back against the suit of armour left over from *Joan of Arc*, Tarra with a firm grasp on his jousting stick. She was eighteen at the time and as dizzy as a merry-go-round. Jen, the Royal's hard-as-nails lesbian barmaid, affectionately referred to Alastair as 'The Man-Slut' and said that he'd try and screw anything without balls.

The rain let up a bit and they set off again. Karen could almost imagine that they were running together through the streets of Paris. Her flat, however, was not behind Notre Dame but behind a high hedge, now waterlogged and slumping. She led Alastair down the path which had been shrunk to a bush track by overgrown rhododendrons. The wide leaves slapped wetly at their coats and legs and flicked back, spraying, after they had passed. Alastair went first and did not seem to notice that Karen was soon drenched. There was no outside light and only a faint glow from the flat upstairs where, every Saturday night, a Christadelphian couple made crucifix-shaped candles that were for sale at the Sunday craft market.

Karen stepped into the darkened doorway and felt Alastair crowd in behind her. The leather of his coat creaked and rubbed against her back and his breath clouded around her. Karen's key took longer to find than was strictly necessary as she waited for his hand to slip around her waist.

'Can't you find it? I'm bloody freezing.'

'No. Here it is.'

She began to apologise even before she was in the door and flicking on the light. 'Sorry, I told you it wasn't much.'

The doorway opened directly into the lounge which also contained the tiny kitchen. The house, like the land, had been divided into more economical units and this had once been the dining room. The carpet by the door was faded and worn to the thread, and the musty smell of trapped damp and mouse piss mixed with the wax fumes from the Christadelphians.

'This is great. You're a real princess. Don't know what I would have done if you hadn't helped me out tonight.'

She was a princess. She waited for him to close the gap between them, to squeeze his puffy lower lip against her mouth, to cup one buttock in his hot hand.

'So is this where I'll be sleeping?' He sat and bounced experimentally on the couch. Bouncing was good. Bouncing was promising.

'I guess.' She moved to join him.

'Have you got any blankets?'

'Oh, yes.' She went to the cupboard by the hot-water cylinder. 'Here. These should be warm enough.' She stood close.

'That's great. The bathroom . . .?'

'Oh, it's through there.' She paused. 'That's my bedroom in there. Through that door. That one.'

'Okay. I'll try not to disturb you.'

'Okay. Though I'll probably be awake for a while.' She waited. 'If you need anything just call out.'

'Great. Right. Good night then.'

'Do you want a drink?' she asked quickly. 'I've got some red wine.' Karen imagined them sitting and talking about his family, the time he cut his knee playing (down by the river? on a family picnic? during a spirited game of bull-rush with the older brother/sister/cousin he always secretly envied?). They would discover a common love for Thai/Greek/seafood before she subtly brought the conversation round to old dalliances, sexual preferences.

'No thanks. I'm buggered. Titus is a really draining part.'

'Okay . . . Good night then.'

'Good night.'

Karen went to the bathroom and then to her room where she reluctantly closed the door. Behind her she could hear Alastair making up the couch and the creak of his leather jacket as it was thrown over a chair. He obviously didn't want to rush her. But she knew it was only a matter of time before he came to her. She had to be ready. She pulled a stick of incense from its packet — *Nubian Nights* — and lit it. The smoke drifted in circles towards the high ceiling where the light from the shaded bulb did not quite reach. The room was cold so she turned on a small bar heater by the bed.

She imagined Alastair flinging open the door, striding purposefully into the room, his blue eyes fixed on her. What to wear? In winter she usually wore an old T-shirt, pink from being in the washing machine with the colours, and serviceable knickers. On cold nights like this she also tended to pull on thick woollen socks. From the back of her bottom drawer she dragged out a black teddy, satin with white possum fur around the cleavage and the hem. It had been a twenty-first gift. Her friends had pooled their money to buy it from the Cupid's Lounge Adult Boutique. Karen slipped it on. It was now too tight around the shoulders and bust and the straps dug into her skin. She felt that if she leaned forward with any suddenness the flimsy material would rip. Still, better than nothing (to begin with anyway).

The room still smelt musty and wax fumes seeped down through the sagging ceiling. She could hear the Christadelphians moving above her. It bothered her. There was nothing as unsexy as a Christadelphian. She lit another four incense sticks, poking them into the dry dirt at the base of a dying peace plant, and slid a tape into the tape deck by her bed. Everything But The Girl started to sing quietly about two lovers who had known each other since they were children. The rumblings of the Christadelphians faded into the distance.

At first Karen lay on top of the sheets as she listened for Alastair's footsteps outside the door and the rattle of the doorknob. Because of the tight teddy she was forced to lie slightly rigid, like someone stiff with the early symptoms of meningitis. Were the curtains better drawn or open? Karen got up awkwardly and closed them. She lay down. And then got up and opened them again. In the end she opted for a compromise — one drawn, the other slightly open. The warmth from the bar heater did not reach her. It rose up to the high ceiling where it gathered like water filling an empty swimming pool on the other side of the world.

At last the cold drove her under the covers where she experimented with the position of the quilt. First up by her chin — 'mock surprise and innocence' — to mostly off her body — 'ready and willing'. In the end, she pulled it around her shoulders — 'warm'. She could always yank it alluringly lower when she heard the door begin to open. It was only a matter of time before Alastair came to her. Karen concentrated on the sound of Tracy Thorn spreading her tears all over town and imagined how it would be. She could feel Alastair's hand on the back of her neck. His manly weight pressing down on her. She smiled and, closing her eyes, surrendered.

In the morning the light coming past the half-open curtain fell across her face. The heater had been on all night and the room was stinking hot and muggy. The air was thick with incense, and the straps of the teddy had cut off the circulation to the tops of her arms which had turned a motley blue. In the lounge the couch was empty. She stared down at the blankets which lay on the floor like a discarded skin. Karen pulled her dressing gown closer across her chest. Her last two eggs had been taken from the fridge. She saw no evidence that they had been cooked and eaten for breakfast. He had simply taken them to eat later. A carton of milk stood empty on the stained bench.

Lying on the green Formica table was a note. It had been written on a page torn from her new *Woman's Weekly*. The headline announced the 10 BIGGEST TURNOFFS OF ALL TIME! and next to it in the margin:

Eternally grateful. You're a princess.
Love and kisses. A.

Karen felt suddenly and overwhelmingly used.

During the rest of the season of *Titus Andronicus*, Alastair was friendly to her but never seemed able to stay for long and chat. He began an affair with the woman playing Tamora. Tamora was married to the Emperor Saturnicus — both in the play and in real life. She had flaming red hair, legs like sticks and skin the colour of chalk.

Night after night, Karen remained in her lighting box behind the tinted glass. In some performances, discerning audience members noted a dimness around the area of the stage where the actor playing Titus was standing. Wasn't there a noticeable murkiness during his big speech in Act 3 Scene 2? Sometimes, when he was not the focus of attention, the actor could be seen frowning up at the lights as though looking for a blown bulb. But overall everyone agreed the production was excellent. One respected critic even wrote that it 'would not be out of place in the West End'. The review was blown up on to A3 paper and taped to the door of the actors' dressing room with the most glowing phrases highlighted in yellow marker.

Nothing was said by the other actors about Karen's slight lapses with the lighting. After all, their lighting was just fine.

Like wallpaper

You can picture it all.

You will meet your father, for the first time in twenty-seven years, at the supermarket. The bright fluorescent lights, the stark canyons of tinned and bottled food. It is the perfect place for an emotional ambush.

Your father will be reaching for a tin of Watties spaghetti with meatballs. You, his cast-aside son, will be holding a jar of artichoke hearts. It will be a small victory. You will have the culinary as well as the moral high ground. You will both stare for a moment, your blue-grey eyes meeting his. With a slightly melodramatic touch, you imagine that time will seem to stop, to freeze solid like the block of ice cream at the bottom of your trolley. Maybe it will.

And then he will turn away. Perhaps it will be to place his spaghetti in the basket he is carrying before turning back to you. Perhaps he will just be turning away, not knowing who he has just met.

'Excuse me,' you will say calmly. (You have, after all, practised saying it a thousand times in front of the mirror.) 'I believe that you are my father.'

Maybe it is then that time will freeze. Solid as ice cream. Hard and silver as the metal bars of the trolley. Still as a photograph.

Your mother is a methodical woman, neat and exact in her movements. On the day she discovers that your father's side of the wardrobe is empty, that his tools are gone from the garage, she takes a sharp knife with a thin blade and eases it between the backs of photographs and the heavy black paper of the family album. You rest your elbows on the edge of the Formica table and cup your chin as she works. Each photograph comes free with a sound like water dripping from a tap. A faint plopping. You are only six but you sit still, fascinated. There is the same tightness in the air that you have noticed before it rains.

When she has done all four corners, your mother places the selected photograph on the neat pile by your elbow. You watch her choose some, leave others, until the pattern becomes clear. Your mother is removing, slicing out, all the photographs that have your father in them. Even if he was just one of many people in a group. There is a picture at a barbecue where he is grinning, holding a brown bottle of beer by the neck at the edge of a crowd. His face is tanned, his hair is blonder than you have ever seen it. This one too is cut free and joins the pile. They all go. Even if your mother is in the photograph with him. All but one of the wedding photographs are surgically removed. Your mother alone in a white dress. Shipwrecked on the empty black page.

The pile by your elbow grows. Your father as a baby. As a boy. Your father on the boat to England, crossing the equator dressed as a cannibal with a bone in his hair. Dancing, working, frowning in a white fisherman's jersey, holding you as a baby. On some pages of the album there are no photographs left. Only the empty spaces marked out like barren sections by the waxy smudges where the corners have been.

Sitting there at the table with the knife in her hand, your mother looks as fragile as the paper people holding hands in a chain over your bed. If you were to blow on her she would flutter and fly away.

Nothing is left to chance in your imagination. Even the setting across from the tinned fruit and vegetables is carefully thought out. The black-eyed peas will stare your father down. The asparagus spears will prick his conscience. Even the photographs of the two plums in light syrup will remind him of the balls he didn't have when it came to sticking with his wife and son. And if he tries to ignore you, tries to brush past and feign ignorance of who you really are, then . . . then the supermarket is perfect.

He will be boxed in by the bulk-buy bins. Cornered by the pyramid of cut-price cat food. In the deli his dark hair will stand out among the hard cheeses and rows of pale, wrinkled uncooked chickens. There will be no hiding among the bags of potato chips or the bottles of Coke in red uniforms standing in military rows almost up to the ceiling. No warm sanctuary among the bags of frozen vegetables.

Finally, he will be trapped by the blue-coated checkout women who will glare at him darkly. Checkout women know what it is like to be a deserted mother. They have got up in the night to check a sick child and returned to a cold bed. They know about men who have taken themselves out of the picture. Know what it feels like not to have the father of their child around.

It is only when your mother carries the pile of photographs out to the yellowed lawn at the back of the council house that you understand what she intends to do. Unconcerned by neatness now, she throws them in a pile and they slip and slide across each other. Then she takes a box of matches from her apron and sets them on fire. A hundred father-faces curl, blacken and burn.

The chemicals in the photographs make the flames flare red and purple, blue and green. There is no wind but the grass is dry and the flames creep out from the central pyre, scorching the ground until you stamp them down. Your mother does not move. Does not even step back from the flames when they threaten to catch her dressing gown on fire. She stares as your father crinkles into nothing.

It is only now that you see the necessity of memory. With no photographs the images in your head are all that you have left of your father, and already you can feel them fading like a coloured shirt soaking in bleach.

You watch as a piece of photograph no thicker than a layer of skin lifts off. The hot air carries it up high, higher than the lemon tree and then up even higher. For a long time you imagine that your father's face can still be seen smiling off into the blue sky.

Your father always said that you had a good imagination.

The question of how you will know him is problematic. You think that you will just *know*. In the same way that you know a blatant lie. But on other, more pragmatic days you imagine a certain way of walking, a tilt of the head that you will instantly recognise as he listens to Tom Jones sing about the green green grass of home through the supermarket speakers. Your home, you will inform him, had a barren patch in the middle of the back lawn where the grass never grew back.

You study yourself in the mirror. You are looking for facial features that are not your mother's. Your mother's maiden name was Bartle. Your father is a Ricketts. You try to ignore Bartle, isolate by elimination everything that is Ricketts. Your eyes are rounder than your mother's, although they are the exact same shade of blue-grey. Your chin is, you see, more prominent. Does your mother have that slight gap between her teeth? Your hair is dark. Hers is light.

It is like doing a jigsaw puzzle in reverse. You are taking pieces away, hoping that you will be left with something significant. The picture on the front of the box. Not a Provence garden scene or spotted puppies playing from *101 Dalmatians*. Your father's face.

You play this game for hours. For days and weeks and months. For years.

Your mother never talks about your father. Never mentions him, not even in passing. She never replies or even looks at you when you ask about him. It is as though she never married him. As though he was never here. Never left shaving foam peppered with whiskers around the bottom of the sink. It is as though your memories are just imagination.

Back in front of the mirror you see that your face is becoming squarer, losing its baby roundness. You have begun to shave. You like shaving. It shows that your face is becoming more like his. That the pieces of the jigsaw are shifting in your favour.

With foam on your face, you locate the almost invisible scar under your left eye where you were bitten by the neighbour's dog when you were nine. When you meet again you will tell your father that you cried for him to come and make it stop hurting. You don't remember if you did or not. You might have.

You will stand directly behind him in the checkout line. You will look around, wondering if people are taking it for granted that you are father and son. The resemblance will now be obvious. (Your diligence in front of the mirror will have been rewarded.) They will think you are a father and son out shopping together. They will think that you are both going back to your house for dinner with your wife and children, or out to a movie. Just a man and his father. After all, the family that plays together stays together.

He will be shopping for one. A basket, not a trolley. Nestled in the bottom will be some cheap bacon or maybe chops, half a dozen large eggs, frozen peas, white bread and instant coffee. You watch as his shopping passes over the red eye of the machine, which beeps in surprise at the 1950s fare.

You half expect him to run but he waits patiently by the SPCA food bin as your shopping is loaded into plastic bags. He will look old.

You have a paper round after school and work for Mr Lee

the milkman on Saturday and Sunday and save enough money to buy your first camera when you are twelve. It is a Pentax ME Super, slightly old even then. You have only the one subject. Men between the ages of thirty-five and fifty.

You photograph them wherever you can find them. On the streets, in parks, standing in groups outside pubs and rugby games, leaving office buildings. You do not ask permission. Suddenly the boy with the camera is there and then he is gone. The photographs have a raw, instant look. Men laughing, arguing, staring blankly, half turning as they see you out the corner of their eyes. Men in hats and suits. Bald men and men with hair. Men with lined faces and smooth-faced men.

You have never really known your father's first name and your mother will not tell you. Will go silent for days when you ask. She has not remarried. Will not even speak to a man unless she has to, and then only 'yes' and 'no'. As you grow older her distrust seems to spread to you like a stain. She avoids your room.

You spend most of your money on getting the photographs developed and, later, on the chemicals and equipment you need to develop them yourself. When you are sixteen you turn your bedroom into a darkroom. The black-and-white photos you pin to the walls. They spread out like a living thing, growing bigger and bigger. Some overlap, but always the man's face is visible. You stare at them before you go to sleep at night. The eyes and the ears and the mouths and chins. Are they like your own? Which one is he?

As more and more photographs are added they entirely cover first one wall and then the others. Like wallpaper.

Outside it will be raining. Perhaps just getting dark. And there will only be a few cars left in the vast car park. Very film noir. You imagine that you are Humphrey Bogart and your father is Claude Rains walking across the tarmac at the end of *Casablanca*. Will this be the beginning of a beautiful friendship?

The rain will smear the reflection of you and your father in the window of your car. He will notice that it is late model and expensive although he will say nothing.

Inside you will both sit in silence. It is a silence that you have imposed. It is not up to him to speak. The rain will beat on the roof and run down the windows. Sitting that close you will smell him and remember riding down the hallway on the tops of his shoes. Wrapping your arms around his legs while he walked stiff-legged with monster strides. You will remember laughing until you had to go and pee.

He may ask you if he can smoke. You will say that you would prefer it if he didn't. You are in charge now. It is in your hands whether to take or to give.

Toys are scattered over the back seat.

'I see you've got children?'

'Yes.' The word grandfather will be avoided.

And you will tell him that they are good boys, that you are a good father. A better father than he was. And it will be as though you have punched him.

And then it will truly begin.

You are eighteen. From all the hundreds of photographs on the walls you have selected three. These are the finalists, the shortlist for the vacancy that has opened up in your life for the position of father. You take them and pin them in a line on the ceiling over your bed so that you can lie back, hands behind your head, and stare at them. For hours and days and weeks. For years.

The one on the left you call Ted. (You think that your father's name had a hard sound, a 't' or a 'd'.) He definitely has your round eyes. His hat is tilted to one side and he is staring into the camera, posing for the boy. On the back is written: *1981, Parker Street Tavern. 12.30pm. Eyes blue.* All the photographs have the place and time written on them in case you finally decide that *he* is the one. In case you need to go back and find him again.

You are now uncertain of the one in the middle, Don. He is in profile and looks right, but he has an old scar that creases his face from his cheek bone almost down to his jaw. You are sure that you would remember the scar even over the ocean of twelve years. It is possible, however, that it happened after he left. But on this particular day you are sceptical.

Dave is your favourite. You want him to be your father. He is standing next to the trunk of a plane tree, its bark mottled and peeling. His face is lined from sun, smiling. He has seen you and he is smiling down on you now. You look for recognition in his eyes. *1983, Walker Park. 5pm.* Dave's hand is in view, leaning against the tree. His fingers are long like yours. His hair is dark and wavy.

By the time you are twenty his is the only photograph left. You place it in a frame on the bedside table.

It is this face that you use when you imagine your father.

Several days, or maybe it will be weeks later, he will turn up at the studio. You will be busy arranging a family group, tilting a daughter's head towards the light or placing a rolled magazine in the father's hand. You will ask Linda to tell him to wait.

As you are saying goodbye to the family, shaking hands and reassuring them that the proof-sheets will be ready within the week, you will see him. He will be sitting in the corner of the reception area, not reading a magazine but just sitting. Watching you. His face will be clean-shaven, scrubbed Kodachrome red. His wavy hair will be smoothed down.

He was in the area, he will tell you, and just popped in for a chat, perhaps some lunch if you're not too busy?

'Why not?' you will say.

You will eat sushi in the park. He has not tried it before, but does not complain. Says, perhaps, that he quite likes it. You are still deciding whether you will warn him about the wasabi.

You are unsure of how the conversation will go after that. What will happen? Will you talk like old friends? Like father and son? Or will the only sound be the laughter of families drifting over from the children's playground? You have been to the park many times, trying to see how it will be. You are here now.

The bench is cold and there are not many people around. The light is fading. Two teenage boys in heavy coats walk towards the toilet block. They eye you wearily.

You imagine your father sitting next to you on the bench. Your old camera is in its brown leather case between you. The face you have chosen for him comes into view like a partially developed photograph slowly appearing from the bottom of the tray.

You can see him now. Can see Dave's face. Can project your father into a probable future full of happiness. You smile.

You can picture it all.

Dreams of a suburban Mercenary

These days I care about very little and look
forward to even less. The best of it is when
the nurse changes the sweat-soaked sheets
or the chaplain with the frozen eye drops by to talk,
although I imagine that I am poor company. I cannot
concentrate for long enough to hold a proper conversation.
I drift in and out of uneasy sleep. My particular sandman
wears a white doctor's coat and visits this hospice bed
often, dispensing a heady mixture of painkillers and false
cheer. But the dreams he brings me are not soothing. They
are nearly always the same: full of faces from my past
swimming into view and then flicking away like fish in a
tank. And, of course, there is always the fat man.

*I see him walking towards me out of the darkness. He is still a fair
way off but I know without doubt that it is him. I hear the hollow
thump of the explosion, as loud as when I heard it that first time.*

I feel the ground shake and see the metal fragments rain down like jagged snow on to the dry grass. The laughter of old people echoes all around me. In my dream the fat man raises his walking stick in cheery greeting.

You can believe my story or not, I say to the chaplain as he sits by my bed. I would understand if you didn't but it's nothing to me one way or the other. Not at eighty-seven. Not here in this penultimate place, this staging post between the hospital and the cemetery. Others will tell you differently, wild fanciful stories, but don't listen to them. The ones who are living at Calbourne Courts now are newcomers. They know only what they've been told, sometimes second or third hand. They've only been shown the dimpled and chipped concrete walls in Unit 14 and the faded bloodstain that looks like a flower on the concrete path. They weren't there when it happened. The chaplain nods his head and smiles as though I am a feverish child. One eye looks over my left shoulder in the direction of the window.

Calbourne Courts Retirement Village sat — sits I should say — at the end of a short cul-de-sac in what has become an unfashionable part of the city. In that summer's hot nor'westerlies litter blew across the mouth of Calbourne Drive, paint slowly peeled and engines revved. After midnight the residents lay beneath thin sheets and listened to the thumping bass of car stereos come closer and then fade away. There were eighteen units in all, although two were vacant at the time, cleared out first by the ambulance and later by the furniture-removal men. I lived in number 15 which, like all the rest, faced into the yellowing central lawn, criss-crossed with cracked concrete paths.

Four rooms. A lounge big enough for a two-seater couch, a chair and a television set. A single bedroom. A bathroom with a shower box lined with a lumpy rubber mat, and a toilet with a handrail. There was also a tiny kitchen with a sink and a stove for those who still did their own cooking. There were meals-on-wheels for the rest. All the units were painted Desert Cream and Seashell Pink over cost-efficient concrete-block walls.

Calbourne Courts was where you went when your husband or wife of forty years died. When your middle-aged sons and daughters kindly informed you that the family home was too much for you now. When you weren't quite ready for dormitory beds and white nurses carrying trays of mashed food, or for a more transitory place like St Mary's where I currently spend all day on my back drug-dreaming about the past.

I watch Mrs Munro stiffly picking up the slender brown off-casts from the cabbage tree outside her window. The onset of Parkinson's disease makes her move like a plastic doll. It is hot and she wears a thin summer dress with small yellow flowers dotted across it.

When she looks up they have surrounded her. There are three young men and they demand cash. When she objects, they push and pull at her until she falls. They are tugging at her paste pearls and taunting her with voices like magpies.

She holds up her hands to ward them off. The skin is rice-paper thin and just beneath the first swollen knuckle is a flash of diamond ring. The three squawk and peck at her. One of them grasps her hand and pulls. The skin beneath the ring is wrinkled and pink, the skin of a baby mouse. It bleeds easily.

They run laughing across the lawn. Mrs Munro's eyes over-flow behind her heavy glasses, and the water catches between her

*lenses and the folded skin of her face and builds up like a
swimming pool.*

I tell the chaplain that Mrs Munro was not able to give
a clear description. The policeman explained, in the
borrowed tone of a patient parent, that half the youths
in the area were skinny and wore their hair short.
Considerably more than half wore clothes that needed a
good wash. What could they do except warn people to lock
their doors at night, and promise that a patrol car would
cruise the area whenever possible?

Despite these precautions, the three returned on
several occasions. They took to wearing black balaclavas
over their almost bald heads. Only their eyes were visible
as they carried away Mr Gardener's television set. Only
their sneering mouths could be seen as they pocketed Mrs
Taylor's ivory brooch, given to her as a present by a second
cousin of the Queen. Their eyes laughed and their mouths
jerked and twitched as I watched them trample Mrs
Littlewood's tiny vegetable garden with heavy boots. You
see, she had nothing valuable to take. Her courgettes paid
the ultimate price for her poverty.

*Old people crowd around, they push into the small room, shuffle
into my field of vision. A meeting has been called. Voices chatter
like temple monkeys.*

*'It's only a matter of time before someone's killed,' says Mrs
Munro. As the very first victim she prides herself on being
something of an expert. There is a mutter of agreement, a clicking
of tongues. It echoes in my head.*

'But what can we do about it?'

'We can lock our doors.'

'What?'

'We can't hide inside all day like rabbits in a burrow.'

'There's nothing we can do.'

'What? Speak up! I can't hear!'

'Be quiet! Be quiet all of you!' Mrs McDonald rolls forward in her wheelchair which makes a gentle electric whirr. 'Listen to all of you clucking like a lot of chickens afraid of the cat.' Her face is collapsed and small like an apple that has sat in the fruit bowl for far too long. Her ears, too big for her face, have lobes that dangle beneath the overhang of her perm. 'The police can't help us, that much is plain.' There is a chorus of agreement. 'We need to get help. We need to get someone who's not afraid to put these young thugs in their place.' She pauses for effect. 'Maybe break an arm or two.'

Everyone stares at her. Mouths normally half open, open wider.

'But that's . . . !'

'We can't . . . !'

'You'd never . . . !'

Mrs McDonald holds up her hand until there is total silence. 'I know a man.'

Mrs McDonald's husband had been in the army's motor-pool and later taken a keen interest in the sometimes shady world of horse-racing. Friends of friends had been contacted. Friends of friends made calls to old acquaintances who owed them favours. They in turn picked up their receivers and dialled. The word of Mrs McDonald's need had trickled down through the city like water through dense soil. Two days after her first call she had a name.

There was another meeting where she told us everything that she knew. That he was an ex-soldier. A hard man. A man who knew that violence had to be met with violence. That the meek inherited bugger all. The word mercenary was never said, but it hung in the air of number 6 Calbourne Courts like tobacco smoke. It stained the pink walls an altogether darker shade.

It was Mrs McDonald and Mrs Harwood who went to meet the man. Mrs McDonald had been the obvious choice to represent Calbourne Courts. Mrs Harwood's inclusion had, however, been the subject of vigorous debate. At sixty-two she was the youngest resident of the retirement village and so lacked a certain standing in the community. Some saw her taste in bright summer frocks as too ostentatious, the hems too short by half. I myself considered it unseemly in a woman of advanced years to flaunt her legs — even if they were the legs of a woman twenty years younger.

I am uncertain of how they travelled, although I knew once, I'm sure. I remember that some of us gathered in the car park to see them off and wish them luck. Perhaps they were on foot. Or rather Mrs Harwood was. Mrs McDonald would have rolled along in her wheelchair over the hot ground. They left us like the Boers trekking down through Africa. Or is that fanciful nonsense? Perhaps I do recall a taxi with a device on the roof for the wheelchair. I prefer to imagine that they moved slowly through the suburbs under the hot summer sun, pioneers searching for sanctuary through shimmering air. It could have happened that way.

I know that I am dreaming but cannot wake myself. He walks towards me, close enough now that I can make out the brown plastic buttons on his cardigan. The darkness is lifting and I can see that there is a faint stain near the left-hand pocket. He is so big that he rolls slightly as he walks, in the same way that a calm ocean rolls in to the shore. I cannot bring myself to look down at his hands. I am afraid of what I will find there. I know that his coming is a good thing, but I fear his arrival.

The chaplain is sitting by my bed. I do not remember him arriving or sitting down, but there he is anyway. I continue telling him my story. Mrs Harwood herself told me the rest, I say. He nods and his bad eye roams around the room. No matter. I want to finish my story. As much for my own sake as for his. She told me how they were surprised that the address they had been given was a modest state house, nothing more than a two-bedroom box painted cream, with fly-spotted venetian blinds in the window. She said that they found him mowing the lawn. He was moving in straight lines, every now and then bending awkwardly to pull out weeds. Mrs McDonald described him to me as portly. When I saw him myself later, I thought him fat. But of course the thing that struck them most was his age. Mrs McDonald's scratching voice drifts to me over the years: 'Seventy-five if he was a day!'

I will not pretend to know the ins and outs of their conversation. A few details told to me come back now. That he used a walking stick with a shiny knotted handle. That his house was pleasantly cool after the summer heat. He rolled a cigarette while they talked but did not light it. She said that his breath smelt of peppermints.

He is closer than before and as fat as I remember. His hair is white and his goatee beard neatly trimmed. His beard has been left to grow in a thin line down the edge of his face, framing an otherwise borderless expanse of skin. He limps toward me through the fog. His voice comes to me as if over a great distance, and it is deep and soothing.

'I fought in Crete and at Tobruk. Don't be fooled. It's not how young or strong you are. It's the intent that matters. The willingness to hurt or kill before they do the same to you. That's all violence really takes — the will.'

By all accounts the negotiations went on for some time. The residents had agreed to put in a hundred dollars each, but the fat man wanted more. How much more I cannot remember, but enough. They haggled. By the time Mrs Harwood and Mrs McDonald were finally led to the front door, things had been settled. A price had been agreed, the bulk of the money payable on completion of the job.

Out on the street Mrs McDonald observed that the fat man grunted and huffed a lot for a soldier of fortune. She personally thought that the three young thugs were going to make mincemeat of the old fool. Mrs Harwood said nothing. She later told me she was thinking about the way that, as they went out the gate, he patted her fondly on the buttock. She could still feel his large warm hand through the cotton of her summer frock.

Three hooded youths walk boldly across the lawn. It is almost midday and the bone-dry grass bends and snaps beneath their feet. We have been told to wait inside and out of sight, but of course we watch. Curtains twitch and watery eyes are pressed to hidden slits.

A newly polished oak clock sits on the small side-table just inside the open door of number 14, next to it a set of silver cutlery still in its box. Heavy boots kick up dust. A tattooed knuckle clenches. Laughing, they push into the darkness of the unit, looking for more. Of course I was not inside, but in my imagination he rises stiffly from a La-Z-Boy to greet them.

'Aah, you've come at last.' His voice would have been calm.

The three are not afraid. They laugh at him. They sneer.

'Where's your cash, you fat old bastard?' The tallest advances, reaching out his hands. His fingers seem to stretch and grow. Before he can touch the fat man there is a blur of movement in the half light and something hard and heavy strikes the side of the hooded boy's knee. He collapses cursing at the old man's feet. His groans echo around my head. Is that a stick the fat man is holding? It is hard to see. Perhaps a heavy crowbar, the end a snake's forked tongue.

The other two stand still like bald statues silhouetted in the doorway. They look uncomprehendingly at the old man standing over their companion. I'm sure there is a moment when they think about running. I can see it in their eyes, as big as my mother's dinner plates. But they are young and he is old. And then one of them reaches into his pocket and pulls out a knife. With a practised flick of his wrist he has it open.

'Wait!'

The fat man's voice commands attention. It freezes them.

He reaches into his own pocket and pulls out something round. At first I think it is a piece of fruit, a lemon or a young pineapple. 'You may recognise this from movies.' His voice is that of a teacher, as though what he is saying is for their education. He moves forward so that they can get a better look. 'It is a hand grenade. A little souvenir I picked up from my time in Africa.'

'That's fuckin bullshit. That's not a real grenade.'

'I thought you'd say that, which is why I've prepared a little demonstration.' Casually he pulls the pin and throws it aside. I hear it strike the edge of the television, watch it slowly spin as it falls.

I can imagine how it must have been. The grenade would have landed on the green carpet between them. I like to think that there was a sudden sharp smell of urine as someone pissed their pants. At the fat man's feet the moaning figure would have pulled off his balaclava as he managed to stand. He ran, tripping and falling. The two others turned and fled with him. From my window in number 15 I saw them go.

They were halfway across the lawn when the grenade exploded. It made a hollow thump like a single strike on a large skin drum. The windows of number 14 blew out, and glass and fragments of metal ricocheted off the walls and landed on the grass like lethal snow, kicking up a low cloud of dust from the dry ground.

When I picked myself up I saw the three running, stumbling, sprawling in their haste. One of them tripped on the edge of the concrete path, leaving a bloody mark from a nasty shrapnel wound in his shoulder, the blood spreading like a rapidly opening bloom. And as they ran a noise began in the units of Calbourne Courts. I still hear it in my dreams.

It echoes off the pink concrete walls and reverberates through the four rooms of each unit until it spills out into the dry courtyard where it collects and swells. It is the laughter of old people. It is loud. Louder perhaps than I can stand. The sound pushes the three running figures like a vengeful wave, jostles and prods them down Calbourne Drive until they are out of sight.

Perhaps it is my memory, perhaps the painkillers the nurse gives me in larger doses every day, but the details shift like the air over the hot tarseal of the car park where we waved goodbye. I seem to remember the fat man emerging from number 14, victorious, unscathed, having been protected by the thick block walls between the lounge and the bedroom where he took refuge. It may be that a party was given in his honour and that Mr Baxter played the accordion and Mrs Munro sang 'The White Cliffs of Dover' four times. I do think I remember something of the sort, although I cannot be sure. Perhaps that was another occasion, a ninetieth birthday which I am mixing up in my mind. Why do I think that it was at that same party that the fat man claimed Mrs Harwood of the summer frocks and the younger woman's legs? Perhaps they really did depart to sail the sheltered waters of the Bay of Islands in his schooner. Perhaps they are there still.

I can no longer say with any certainty what is true. I do, however, have an image in my mind of a man walking towards me along Calbourne Drive. I can see him now, when I close my eyes. He is a fat man and uses a stick, and in his other hand is something like a cricket ball or a piece of fruit. This seems real but who can say? Who can be certain of anything these days? I am sure he remembers what truly happened better than I do. I will be sure to ask him when he finally arrives.

The Distant Man

ONE

The Jade Garden is an arrangement that he has drifted into with his father. On the first Monday of every month he drives into the centre of the city. It is only a short journey from the gallery where he works, ten minutes, never more than fifteen even in the worst extremes of weather or city traffic. He leaves his car in a parking building and takes the narrow lift with its faint smell of urine down to the street. From there five minutes' leisurely walking will see him approaching the restaurant.

The exercise is pleasant after the inactivity of a morning spent sitting in his office. He savours the gentle working of his muscles, the easy swing of his arms, the undoing of cricks. Part of his route follows the curve of the river past the arched war memorial with its two stone lions, and in summer he walks along the neatly mown bank beneath the willow trees where the light is dappled. Of course he thinks of the impressionists but, more readily, of a favourite work by Evelyn Page and another by Bill Sutton from the late '50s. If it is raining he keeps to the footpaths, carries an umbrella and listens to the percussion of the rain on the taut fabric. Regardless of the weather, he times his journey to arrive at the Jade Garden at 12.30 precisely.

His father, Jack, is always waiting at the top of the flight of steps that leads up to the main door. A tall, gaunt man of seventy-two, his slightly hunched stance is distinctive even from a distance, a question mark on the horizon. His father stands in the doorway, framed by red lacquered wood, glancing occasionally along the street towards the river. If there is a breeze, or the day is in any way cool, Jack wears a brown overcoat and faded tartan scarf. He has always been a predictable dresser. His thin hair, which he allows to grow too long, sits above his ears like tufts of raw cotton and moves in the breeze as he waits.

He finds it difficult to know exactly when to acknowledge his father. Too far away and he considers there to be an embarrassingly long wait until they meet. Too close and it looks as though he has been ignoring him. He compromises. He waits until he is just beyond the last plane tree pushing up through the footpath, raises a hand, smiles. His father habitually returns the gesture. As though they are playing a children's game where one has to mirror the movements of the other.

He climbs the flight of concrete steps. They shake hands and go inside.

The Jade Garden was his suggestion. It has a certain ambience, a well-orchestrated tranquillity, he finds pleasing.

The same hostess greets them every month, plastic-coated menus held stiffly up under her arm. She is Asian, young, slim, but with no trace of an accent. He has no difficulty understanding her polite enquiries after their health. He notes how her black hair is pulled back tightly from her forehead without a single hair out of place. If it is winter she takes their coats and relieves him of his umbrella, which she hangs on one of several hooks behind the reception desk before leading them along the red carpet laid out from the door, across the foyer and down the three steps into the restaurant proper.

The Jade Garden comprises a single large room divided into sections by low partitions. It is well heated, never cold even in July and August. The principal colours are gold and red, colours to which he has always been partial. He approves of the way the lighting is kept low and the polished leaves of the peace plants screen the tables one from another. Faint music plays, modern but inoffensive and blessedly devoid of lyrics. An occasional waft of incense, although admittedly a cliché, reaches the diners. On a Monday there are never more than half a dozen other patrons, mostly Asian, and only a few discreet staff.

Their regular table is near the back of the room by the window. On the first Monday of the month it is always available. The reserved sign was not something he requested. It appeared on their fourth visit. Only a small courtesy but nonetheless another reason why he continues to bring his father here.

Their table overlooks a compact courtyard where bamboo has been planted to hide the concrete-block wall in the rear. In the foreground there is a kidney-shaped pond. Four large carp, orange and black, circle slowly, brushing against one another as they turn in the small space. The largest fish has an injury or a deformity. He is not sure which. Its spine is curved at a point just above the tail, giving it a peculiar bent appearance. It swims with ease, however, and shows no signs of distress, circling continuously with the others.

The hostess serves them herself. She makes a show of handing them the menus before taking their drink orders (a glass of Riesling for him, beer for his father), and then retreats to give them time to look at the menu although they are familiar with the selection and have fallen into a pattern of ordering the same food every month. Chicken with cashews for him, pork and vegetables for his father. The rice, which comes in a separate dish, is soft and glutinous.

Over the course of the meal they make conversation. His father talks about current events, things he has read about in the newspaper or seen on the evening news. A disappointing second half in the last All Black test. An upturn in the Kiwi dollar. A spell of unseasonable frost which has burnt the spring bulbs.

He listens politely, drawing his father out with questions and observations of his own, although he finds current affairs and sport uninspiring topics and has no interest in gardening. His father speaks in a quiet voice as though there are people at the other tables who might overhear, cocked ears behind the waxy leaves of the peace plants; as though the information he conveys is somehow sensitive. Jack raises the food to his mouth between topics. He has not mastered chopsticks, giving up on their second visit and opting instead for the fork the waiter never forgets to bring.

He cannot remember a time when conversations with

his father did not deal with the practical, the concrete matters of day-to-day living. Their discussions are never heated or even particularly animated. His father is not a man of passions, he accepts this. Before Jack retired he was a builder. A practical man used to the company of other practical men. It was always his mother who filled the circling silence with her enthusiasms, her sudden exclamations of wonder and outrage, her gossip and trivia, her *joie de vivre*. Her death shifted the focus on to Jack, who often seems lost for words, dumbfounded by the simple act of conversation, left searching for topics and links until he inevitably retreats back to familiar, well-trodden ground.

He makes an effort to keep up his end of the conversation. He shares carefully chosen details of his job. He is the director of the Heaphy Gallery. It is a public art gallery, small by international standards but with a growing reputation. He believes that it is not entirely vanity to claim that the gallery's recent successes have been largely due to his own influence. During his six years as director, the Heaphy has mounted no fewer than seven major exhibitions. A significant number for such a small institution so far off the beaten cultural track. In the last eighteen months alone he has organised a retrospective showing of the work of Ralph Hotere, *Beyond the Black Light*; also an exhibition of the self-portraits of Rita Angus. For the Hotere there were queues out into the street and a complimentary item appeared on the national news, for which he was interviewed against the white marble of the gallery steps.

Watching the news later he had appraised himself as one might appraise a stranger or an unfamiliar painting by a favourite artist. All things considered he was pleased. He saw a tall, well-dressed man in his late forties with a high forehead but not yet balding. With an air of considered experience rather than age. There were inviting lines in the corners of his eyes. He judged himself pleasant, open, neither disconcertingly handsome nor forgettably bland. He spoke slowly, in a well-modulated voice. His answers were to the point.

The exhibition had record attendance figures.

During the lunches with his father at the Jade Garden, however, he tries not to talk about his work too much. He is well aware that his father has no history of art appreciation, no context in which to place the work he does at the Heaphy. He deliberately steers the conversation towards less challenging matters. He talks about family.

He has a younger sister, Joan, who lives in Brisbane. There is a brother-in-law and three young nieces whom he has not seen in several years. Occasional e-mails sent to the gallery keep him updated. It is information that he stores up and passes on to his father. Jack, in his turn, shares any news he may have gleaned from Joan's regular phone calls from Australia.

They also talk about his own son, Richard. He is divorced from Richard's mother. They married young, then divorced quickly when both still in their twenties — something he no longer bothers to regret. Richard is living in Dunedin, is in his first year studying medicine at Otago University. By all accounts he is doing well, is on track for a successful career. His son is not distinguishing himself academically, but he is managing to pass his courses. Richard and he see each other a few times a year and, of course, they speak on the telephone.

He does not look forward to his lunches with his father,

nor does he dread them. A month provides ample material for conversation. He is in the habit of storing ideas, pocketing them so that they can be brought out over the course of the meal, one at a time like souvenirs of a brief sojourn. The ritual of ordering and eating food is sufficiently distracting to fill any awkward silences that may appear.

Generally speaking he does not order any dessert although, depending on how much work he has to get back to, they may request a coffee. For a Chinese restaurant, he finds the coffee surprisingly good. But more often, having finished their meals, he announces that it is time for him to be getting back to the gallery. He has work to do. His father is understanding. They rise and walk back past empty tables to the reception desk.

He always insists on paying for the meal himself. The Jade Garden is very reasonable. Even with coffee, the bill never comes to more than thirty-five dollars. The hostess says goodbye to them and escorts them to the door, opening it gracefully for them to pass through.

Once outside, it is their habit to pause at the foot of the steps. They shake hands again and tell each other to take care. He confirms their meeting for the coming month and they part. He begins the walk back to his car, thankful for the opportunity to walk off his lunch.

The whole meeting takes up only an hour of his time. They have met this way for the five years since his mother died. It is an arrangement that he considers entirely satisfactory.

Until one day. It is the first Monday in October. When he arrives at the restaurant his father is not waiting for him outside. The sight of the empty doorway is so unexpected that for a moment he is flustered. Perhaps he has got the wrong time. The wrong day. But no. The mistake is not his. He stops and looks up and down the street. The day is blustery, the wind swirls, eddying between the tall buildings. Perhaps his father has simply retreated inside to avoid the wind.

Inside the restaurant, however, they have not seen his father. The hostess acts suitably concerned, crinkling the skin of her forehead beneath her straight hairline. She suggests that his father will arrive soon.

'Yes. It is possible that he has missed his bus. I will wait.'

He sits at their usual table and is brought a complimentary cup of green tea from which steam rises into the room. He watches the carp circle. The bamboo shifts in the wind pushing down into the courtyard from above, corrugating the surface of the pond, making it opaque. As he watches, the goldfish appear to melt across the surface of the water like oily stains of orange and white and then regain their solid shapes before the next gust of wind.

Annoyingly he has left his cellphone in his office. After twenty minutes he asks if he can use the telephone and is directed to a small alcove next to the door of the kitchen. There is the smell of fried food as he dials, the sibilant hiss of vegetables landing in hot oil. The phone rings in his father's house but is not picked up. He stands holding the receiver slightly away from his ear. He lets the phone ring for several minutes and then places the receiver back in its cradle.

As he walks back to his car he considers the possibility that his father may be ill. At his age some degree of ill health is inevitable. But he does not think he has any reason to be seriously concerned. Generally speaking, his father is a healthy man — excellent, in fact, considering his age. He is a regular walker, a man who swims at the local pool twice a week. He cannot actually recall the last time his father was ill. Certainly not a likely candidate for the sudden fall that cracks a hip or the scalded hand that will not heal — injuries which, he is aware, often mark the beginning of the end.

But he is at a loss to explain this unprecedented failure to meet at the Jade Garden. And why no call to the restaurant to clarify the situation? He cannot think of any circumstance in his father's life that could be so pressing as to prevent him from keeping their monthly appointment.

His father's house is in a suburb on the hills, in the older part of town where property prices still manage to edge up even in times of recession. The street where he lives angles upwards, climbing a narrow spur, giving the houses a view over the city and up the coast to the north. The old villas and bungalows are tiered one above the other, peering uneasily over each other's shoulders like distant relatives in a group portrait.

The house is a single-storey villa painted white with a pale blue trim around the windows. It is a large house on a large section, a quarter acre in lawns and flower-beds. There is a veranda that wraps around two sides. His father bought it cheaply in the early '70s, before the property booms, and renovated it himself. Too much though now, he believes, for a man of his father's age. But Jack is not willing to talk about selling the house, moving to somewhere smaller. On the two occasions when he has raised the subject, his father has shaken his head like an irritated old horse and refused to discuss it.

He parks his car on the sloping street and walks up a

steep flight of grey concrete steps leading from the wrought-iron gate to the house. The steps give way to a path that curves around the front past rose-beds. There are phlox and lavender by the front door. The edge of the lawn is neatly clipped and a curled garden hose rests to one side of the path.

There is no doorbell so he knocks on the stained glass of the door. No answer. He tries the handle. It rattles loosely but is nevertheless locked. He walks around to the side of the house where geraniums and agapanthus line the path. There is a conservatory here that his father added on to the house himself shortly after he retired, but the sliding aluminium doors are locked. He knocks and puts his face close to the glass, making a visor of his hands. Inside there is a clutter of spider plants and flowering succulents, a cane chair with a high rounded back, a footstool. A book is splayed open on the floor. He knocks on the glass again. His father does not appear, tousled and apologetic.

He stands back and looks around, uncertain of what to do next. He has met a dead end, has exhausted his options.

Because of the slope of the hill he can see over the low hedge into the neighbour's back garden. He watches as a woman emerges from the house next door. She walks in profile to him, carrying a green plastic hamper full of what he thinks are white sheets. In the middle of her lawn is a clothesline, round and spindled like a wind-stripped umbrella. She reaches it and puts the hamper down. For a moment she bends and disappears from his view. When she straightens up he sees that she has in her hand not a sheet but a cloth baby's nappy bleached a pure, somehow startling, white.

He walks over to the hedge.

'Excuse me.'

She starts, a visible jolt as though prodded, and looks around, unable to instantly place the speaker. It is only her head that turns. He thinks that with her long neck, her large eyes, she is like some type of grazing animal. Not a deer. She is too solid in the legs and trunk for that comparison, but certainly something skittish away from the herd.

'I'm sorry,' he says. 'I didn't mean to startle you.'

He guesses that she is in her late twenties. Her pale hair is pulled in to a loose ponytail. She is wearing baggy dungarees, no doubt left over from her pregnancy, and a yellow T-shirt. Her feet are bare on the mossy brickwork beneath the clothesline. She glances furtively towards the house where he imagines her baby is sleeping.

'I'm looking for Mr Alymer. I'm his son, Mark.'

'His son?' she repeats.

'Yes. Have you seen him today?'

He sees her relax. She eases down from the balls of her feet. He can guess what she is thinking. It's all right. This is the son. Family.

'Not since yesterday,' she says. 'I saw him out on the street when I was coming home. About three o'clock. He had some shopping.'

'I was supposed to meet him in town for lunch but he didn't arrive.'

She frowns. 'Do you think he's all right?'

The question forces him to reconsider the option that his father is not all right, that something is seriously wrong.

'I'm sure he's fine. He probably just forgot.' But he knows that this is an easy pretence of the type shared with strangers. In four years his father has never forgotten their monthly meeting. 'Thanks anyway. I'll just have a look around.'

The woman comes to the hedge and watches as he goes back to the conservatory. Nothing has changed there. The glass reflects his own face. He looks puzzled, anxious. He is surprised to see that the book lying on the floor is a biography of the war artist Peter McIntyre. How long has his father harboured an interest in artists, in art?

The woman calls across to him. 'Is there a spare key?'

He turns and sees only her head, balanced on the edge of the hedge like a magician's trick.

'I'm not sure. I'll try around the back.'

He walks behind the house but there is nothing to see there either. There is a double row of stacked firewood leaning against the weatherboards and a chopping block surrounded by pale splinters of wood but no sign of an axe. It is colder in the shadows. The first window he comes to is the bathroom. The glass is bubbled, the opaque of milky water, and he can make out nothing inside. The other window looks through into his father's office. A desk without a computer, a bookshelf, several framed nautical maps on the wall. Everything is neat, tidy. The window resists his attempts to lift it open.

Back at the front of the house he is surprised to see that the woman is now standing on the veranda. She has lost her skittish air and meets his gaze directly. She is taller than he thought, almost as tall as he is. Her feet are still bare and he sees that her toes are long, splayed across the wood as though she is unused to wearing shoes.

'I thought I heard a noise,' she says. She nods her head towards the door. 'Listen.'

They both stand perfectly still. He strains his ears,

leaning his head slightly towards the door, but can hear nothing out of the ordinary. A car goes by on the street, heading down the hill, and the driver turns her head to look at them. He thinks they must make a strange sight, two adults playing stiff candle on the veranda.

'I don't hear anything,' he says.

'It sounded like an animal.' She makes a noise deep in her throat that may or may not mimic the noise she claims to have heard.

There are long rectangles of dimpled stained glass framing the door. Red glass roses grow near the top. The pane he puts his face close to is a darker red, and everything he can see inside is tinged burgundy. The glass is as old as the house and has run, pooling and thickening towards the bottom so that his view of the interior is stretched and distorted. He is looking along a corridor with a polished wooden floor. Rugs have been scattered along its length. There is a plant stand and a narrow table to one side.

It is only when he concentrates on the door at the far end that he sees his father. He is lying on his back on the floor, half in and half out of the bathroom, with only his head and shoulders visible. He is not moving.

'I can see him. There on the floor.' He grasps the door handle, pushing hard. The door rattles in its frame but does not open.

The woman is looking through the glass. He feels her shoulder push against his. 'The key is still in the door.'

She turns suddenly and walks down the steps. What is she doing? He watches her bend and forage under the lavender until she returns holding a half-brick covered in clumps of loose earth. Brown slaters drop on to the boards of the veranda near her bare feet and scuttle in her wake.

Without consulting him, she gives the glass two short taps. There is a surprisingly muted crack and a small shower of red glass scatters inwards on to the polished wood. A single shard falls back on to the veranda and shatters. The woman jumps back from the door, afraid of cutting her feet. Gingerly he reaches in through the hole she has made and turns the key.

It is cool inside and dim. His father is still in his pyjamas. The top is unbuttoned, and his grey chest-hair is matted together as though he has been in the shower or has been sweating heavily. He is embarrassed to see that his father's pyjama pants are down around his thighs and that his penis is exposed. It is pale, bloodless and slack. He does not want the woman to see — for his father's sake, rather than hers. He positions his body between her and his father, and reaches down, pulling the pyjamas so that Jack is covered.

'I'll call the ambulance,' she says, and vanishes.

At the sound of her voice his father's left arm moves slightly. He makes a noise deep in his throat, a primitive gurgle that could be anything: an attempt at speaking, or simply the release of trapped air and phlegm.

He is aware of the woman speaking from the kitchen. She is giving the address to the operator. She says, 'I don't know. We just found him.'

'Stay still,' he says to his father. His voice is little more than a whisper. 'Don't try and move.' He crouches down but does not touch his father. His father's eyes are partly open. They roll slightly beneath the lids. The skin of his face is grey and blotched.

He is not sure what he should do. He has heard that you

should never move a patient yourself. Or is that only for accidents, hit-and-run victims lying bloody in the street?

He stands and goes into the bedroom, searching. The bed has not been slept in. There is a coarse woollen blanket folded in the top of the wardrobe. He brings it back and lays it over his father's body. His bare feet, blue veined and cracked at the heels, poke out.

There is a choking noise like the wet mutter of blocked pipes and his father is throwing up in an unexpected gush on to the blanket. Afraid that his father will choke, he grasps his head and turns it to the side. Fluid, pale yellow and watery, continues to spill out of him, spreading from the outlet of his mouth, over the edge of the rug and on to the wooden floor.

The yellowed vomit, the acidic smell. He stands and steps back. He thinks he might throw up himself, and looks away from the liquid's progress across the wooden floor.

The woman has come back into the hallway.

'He was sick.' He feels foolish for stating the obvious.

'Has he said anything?'

'No.'

She crouches down next to his father, ignoring the sputum soaking into the rug. Before he can stop her she is lifting him. He thinks that she is shifting him into the recovery position, but she moves her body so that she is cradling him. Her arms pass easily under his thin body. When did his father get so thin? She sits on the floor, the old man's head resting on her thigh, smoothing the hair back and across his scalp where the skin is mottled from the sun.

He can think of nothing to do except watch.

She talks to his father in a low voice: sing-song,

nonsense words of reassurance. He wonders if this is the voice she uses with her newborn baby, the night-babble she speaks when her child wakes in the long darkness, as she sits next to the cot before lifting him to her breast?

'Get a tissue or a towel,' she says. 'Something to clean him up.'

He goes to the bathroom, pulls handfuls of toilet paper from the roll. As he turns to leave he sees himself in the bathroom mirror. He looks flustered and his hair is askew. A man in his forties holding a wad of white tissue. For some reason the sight makes him ashamed, as though he has spotted himself in the middle of some act of deviance.

He returns to the hallway and hands her the tissue. He stands looking down at her as she wipes his father's mouth and chin with gentle strokes. When she is finished, she brushes back the thin hair with her hand, moving it away from Jack's forehead. His father stirs in her arms. She hum-talks to him, most of her words not really words at all. She tells his father that everything is fine. That everything is going to be fine. All right. Her voice, no, more her tone, offer shelter.

For a moment his father opens his eyes. He looks up at her face and seems to see her. His expression softens. After a moment his father closes his eyes again and it is almost as though he has chosen to be here. As though he has simply fallen asleep here in the hallway in this woman's arms.

He stands back silently by the wall. He does not think that his father has seen him or is aware of his presence. He feels as though he is intruding on this scene, as though he is a voyeur caught peeking in a neighbour's window.

After a long time he hears the ambulance's siren, faint but clear like a distant keening.

TWO

He waits in a small room in the hospital where he makes tea in polystyrene cups from the machine in the corner. He is the only occupant of the room and has spent his time watching people move past his door and down the corridor: blue-uniformed nurses with quick insect steps and loud laughs; perplexed relatives; doctors; an old woman who spoke polite nonsense to him as she slowly ushered a pole on wheels from which dangled a bulbous bag of yellow liquid. He is just about to find a nurse to again ask about his father when a man appears at the door.

'Mr Alymer?'

'Yes.'

'I'm Danie Peterson. I'm the doctor who's treating your father.' They shake hands. 'Would you come this way please.'

He is led along corridors with paths worn down the middle of the pale orange linoleum. The doctor walks slightly ahead, keeping up a steady stream of small talk. He is South African. Probably one of the recent wave of immigrants who have fled here from the aftermath of apartheid. Thinning blond hair caps a boyish, slightly doughy face. He believes that the man can be no more than thirty.

He is expecting to be taken directly to his father, to turn into a ward and find him propped up in a hospital bed, smiling sheepishly and apologetic for the inconvenience he has caused. Instead, the doctor holds open the door to a small office. There is a desk and a bookcase. Beyond the desk is a window with a view of another wing of the hospital, three-quarters in shadow. Looking across the divide, he can see patients moving around in their rooms.

'Take a seat.'

'Thank you.' He sits, expectant.

The doctor also sits and spreads some papers across the desk but does not refer to them immediately. He comes straight to the point. 'Mr Alymer, your father has suffered an epileptic attack.'

This is unexpected. Will he now be required to force objects between his father's teeth, to bit him like a horse as he writhes on the floor? 'I was not aware that people developed epilepsy at my father's age.'

'They don't normally. In this case I'm afraid the epilepsy is a symptom of an underlying problem. Based on this attack and the other symptoms he has been able to tell us about, we thought it best to perform an MRI. A scan of your father's brain.'

'I see. And what did you find?'

The doctor shifts in his chair. 'I'm sorry to have to tell you but your father has a quite advanced brain tumour.'

So now it is said. Laid out clinically in this doctor's clipped vowels. A verdict not subject to rescission. Brain tumour. Cancer. It is a word that has always seemed to him to be hovering in the air, looking for people to attach itself to. And now it has settled on his father lightly in the night like a large predatory moth.

From a red-and-white envelope on the desk the doctor produces a series of images. A single sheet divided into nine separate photographs. (Are they photographs in the technical sense? he wonders. He is unsure). He sees a curving landscape of rolling hills and valleys, each viewed from a slightly different perspective. He is immediately struck by how beautiful they are. There is the graduation between bone and flesh, between solidity and emptiness and all the numerous combinations in between. The black and whites and the liquid greys. Here is art of a high order. He could frame this sheet and hang it in the gallery today, give it pride of place, possibly even mount an exhibition, and would never have its artistic merit, its profundity, questioned.

The doctor is still speaking. 'This darker mass, here, is the tumour. And here. Do you see?' He finds himself nodding. 'It is relatively large, about the size of a golf ball in real terms.' The man demonstrates by holding up the finger and thumb of his left hand in a broken circle. 'We'll need to do further tests but I'm confident that this is a type of tumour called a glioblastoma multiforma which, I'm sorry to say, is the most aggressive form.'

'I see.'

He decides that he does not like this young South African. This immigrant. There is something too enthusiastic in his manner. The man is inappropriately eager to parade the medical facts.

'This must all be quite a shock. I don't want to overwhelm you with medical jargon.'

'I have six years of higher education, Dr Peterson. I think I can cope.'

The doctor blinks twice. 'Of course. Well, I'm going to recommend that your father is administered a course of a steroid called Dexamethasone. It will relieve some of the pressure that the tumour is creating inside his cranium. That should reduce the severity of his headaches.'

'I was not aware that my father had been suffering from headaches.'

'He told me that he's been having quite severe

headaches now for about —' he checks his notes for the first time — 'six months. He's been treating himself with Panadeine. He's also been having some problems with his eyesight, blurring and some tunnel vision.' He is reading straight from his notes now.

'He's never mentioned anything to me.'

The doctor smiles and nods his head. He finds it a condescending gesture as though the man believes he is privy to a secret. 'Actually it's quite normal for older patients, particularly men, not to discuss symptoms with their families. It's not entirely a cliché when people say that the family are often the last to know.'

'Still. It is a surprise.'

'Of course it is.'

So. His father has been concealing problems with his health. Serious problems, as it turns out. He tries to recall their last meeting. He searches his memory for unexplained lapses in his father's conversation or fleeting expressions of pain which he read nothing into at the time. But the truth is he can remember almost no specific details of their lunches at the Jade Garden. All their meals together are overlaid in his mind, blurred and indistinct like the carp below the wind-ruffled water. It is entirely possible that one of these headaches came upon his father as they sat together spooning white rice on to their plates and that his father did not say a word. And that he himself did not notice.

'Can you tell me what treatments are available. How do you propose to deal with this tumour?'

'Mr Alymer, I'm very sorry to say but there is no treatment that is going to help your father. With many other low-grade tumours we have had good results with surgery and radiotherapy, but these would be pointless in this case. The position of the tumour, here, deep in the left hemisphere, and its quite advanced growth mean that treating it would achieve very little and would undoubtedly reduce your father's quality of life in the time he has left.'

'So you are telling me that his condition is terminal?'

'Yes. I'm afraid so.'

Aah. He sees now. The collapse, this discussion, these are just the first steps along a short and treacherous path. He stares over the doctor's shoulder to the other building. In one of the rooms he can see a woman in a pale blue nightgown. She is standing, framed in the window, carefully removing selected flowers from a vase of what look like irises on the sill.

He brings his gaze back to the doctor who is looking at him expectantly. 'Have you told him this?'

'Yes. I discussed the details with him earlier. In fact, he was the one who asked me to talk to you. He thought you would prefer to hear the news from me. He told me that you would have questions which I could answer.'

'How did he react? I imagine he was quite shocked.'

'Actually, your father was very calm when I told him. But, in my experience, the first reaction is often unreliable. It's only after a few days, when news of a terminal illness has had time to sink in, that people show their true feelings. Some get depressed, some go into denial. Others deal with it remarkably well. It's impossible to tell early on.'

He is aware that the obvious question is still unasked. It is what this interview has been building towards. Across in the far room the woman in the blue nightgown finishes with the flowers and vanishes from view.

'How long would you estimate my father has left to live?'

The doctor frowns, wrinkling the smooth expanse of his forehead. 'There are so many variables in cases like this that anything I say is, of course, just an informed guess.'

'Yes. But in your opinion.'

In the end there is a surgical precision to the way the man delivers his prognosis. 'Anywhere between three and five months. Frankly, I'd be surprised if he lives until Christmas.'

He talks to the doctor for another twenty minutes. They discuss what he can expect to happen to his father over the following months. But he is left with the impression that the actual outcome will be a lottery. It is possible that his father will develop very few symptoms. Alternatively, there may be sudden and sharp decline in the near future. Everything from Jack's speech to his ability to reason could be bulldozed aside by the tumour's advance, by what he is already thinking of as the colonisation of his father's head. Or his father could simply sleep more and more, a slow wilting. He could lose his speech or his sight. A complete personality change cannot be ruled out. Jack could become violent and unruly. In which case he might have to be cared for in a special facility. Possibly restrained.

The doctor pegs out the boundaries. Here. Inside these lines. This is what you can expect.

When he has learnt all he thinks he can for the moment, he thanks the doctor and is directed to Ward 27. The oncology ward. He takes the lift up two levels and follows the signs. He stands in the doorway, watching, taking stock before entering.

His father shares a room with three other men. His bed

is on the left-hand side, closest to the door. He imagines that here, as everywhere, a pecking order exists. It is probable that the longer a man stays in this room, the closer he gets to the window, to the light. But the catch is that only the very sick men stay any length of time. The religious symbolism is not wasted on him. Historically speaking, art often concerns itself with depictions of dying men moving closer to the light.

A nurse is arranging his father's pillows, bullying them into shape with short chops of her hands. He watches from the doorway as his father leans forward, his face stiff with the effort. Jack is wearing a blue hospital gown that bags around the front. He can clearly see the tendons in his father's neck, taut and thin like binding twine. Gaunt. Yes, gaunt is the right word for the new and unexpected way in which the skin moulds to his father's skull, stretching tight over the cheekbones and around the bottom of his jaw. He is reminded of washed-up jellyfish spread over the dry rocks at the edge of the ocean. Something for young boys to poke at with sticks.

Only one of the other men has visitors, four large women in bright floral dresses. He thinks that they may be Samoan — Islanders certainly. They cluster around the bed diagonally opposite his father, next to the window. The man they are visiting lies back on top of the sheets, his head unsupported by any pillow. He is as frail as his visitors are solid. The women seem to ignore him as though they have just bumped in to each other on the street. They laugh at each other's comments loudly with their teeth showing. The room seems full of them.

His father sees him standing half in and half out of the doorway and smiles as though embarrassed to be seen here, as though caught in the middle of some illicit rendezvous.

When the nurse leaves he goes and stands by the bed. 'How are you feeling?'

'Better now. They've given me something for the headaches.'

'Good. I am glad you're feeling better.'

'The doctor said it was you who found me.'

'I got worried when you didn't arrive for lunch.'

'Just as well.'

'Do you remember much?'

'No. Not much. I remember the woman from next door. Just before the ambulance came.'

'That's right. She helped me look for you. She broke the glass in the door so that we could get in.'

He nods slowly. 'I don't know her name. Her husband left her a few months ago, before the baby was born. The house is going on the market.'

There is a pause in their conversation. He does not know how to reply to this. He finds and holds an image of the woman sitting on the floor, cradling his father in her arms. Her bare feet, long toes seeming to grasp the wooden floor. To this image he adds the label of deserted wife and mother.

His father looks over to where the four women are gathered like floats waiting for the Christmas parade to start. He follows his father's gaze. Despite their size and the noise they are making, the man in the bed seems oblivious to his visitors' presence. As oblivious as they seem to him. He lies back, staring blankly up at the ceiling with a hollow face. His skin is the colour of saffron.

'The doctor told me that he's spoken to you about what's wrong.'

His father does not look at him. 'Yes. He's shown me the x-rays.'

He does not correct him.

They discuss practicalities. The doctor has said that there is no reason why Jack cannot leave the hospital after a couple of days. There are some tests to perform, a period of observation, but after that he can certainly return home. The steroids can be administered with a minimum of fuss, a normal life resumed. He introduces the idea of hiring a nurse for a few hours a week, someone who can help around the house and monitor the situation. His father seems receptive, even positive.

He lays everything out for Jack, spreading the possibilities across the white hospital sheets like a quilt. He does not raise the question of how long this new life can be maintained, or of life beyond the short term.

The pillows are so white that his father's head seems silhouetted against them. As he talks he notices that there are small marks, blemishes across the skin, sunspots and old scars, forming faded patterns like Mr Rorschach's ink or the faint view of sand seen through deep water. He half-expects to see some visible effect of the tumour, a swelling perhaps or a darker bruising on the surface of the skin, but of course there is nothing. The tumour is hidden deep beneath the foothills of his father's brain.

From the bed in the corner the four women unexpectedly begin to sing. He stops speaking and looks towards them, as do his father and the men in the other beds. It is a song that rises and dips like a kite, the words in a language he does not understand. He finds himself annoyed and wishes that they would stop. This is not, he thinks, a place for song. There are after all other patients in the ward who may be disturbed by the sound. But the women do not stop. If anything, they become louder.

He thinks their song may, in fact, be a hymn, a sung prayer. It has that feel. An ecclesiastical tempo. The sound washes over the room, rising and falling in a gentle cadence. Several nurses appear, coming one by one to the doorway, where they stand and watch, smiling. No one makes a move to stop the singing.

What is there in this place, he wonders, to sing about? Certainly there are few blessings to be thankful for. All that he can think of is that they are making a supplication. To the God of cancer. To the deity of rapidly multiplying cells and things the size of golf balls. If that is true, then he believes they are wasting their time. Beyond what the doctors are offering he can see no hope for any of the patients here.

He leaves after half an hour, promising to return the next morning. His father is worried about the house.

'I'll get someone to come and repair the glass in the door.'

'And maybe you could leave a few lights on? So that it looks like someone is there.'

'All right. I'll do that.'

His father tells him that there have been several break-ins in the area over the last few months. There is also a cat, a stray, that his father has adopted. It will need feeding. He promises to take care of all the details. As he stands and waits for the hospital lift to arrive, it occurs to him that this will be his life for the next few months. A life held in indentured service to his father's dying.

Once outside, he is surprised to see that it is almost dark. Only the faintest touch of blue remains in the sky.

The river runs past the back of the hospital and on the other side are the botanical gardens. He walks back to his car along a path of crushed stones which crunch loudly beneath the soles of his shoes. On the other bank a man in overalls is working late, herding leaves with a blower into deep drifts in the near darkness.

Further on there is a footbridge on which he stops. Slightly downstream is a small weir. The river passes over a lip and scatters down across concrete into a deep pool. He stands for a long time and listens to the white noise of the water.

And then he is moving away. He walks among the trees' shadows only fractionally darker now than the surrounding night. At the edge of the hospital grounds he comes to a busy road. He stands and waits for a break in the traffic. A turning car swings towards him from a side road, and for a brief moment he is caught, exposed by the white beams of its headlights. He wonders what the driver sees. A fleeting view of a tall thin man standing still in the shadows, framed by the trunks of the trees behind and the branches above him. He crosses the road and again finds himself beneath streetlights. He begins to walk the short distance back to his car.

fish 'n' chip shop song

A one, two; a one two three four . . .

●   VERSE ONE

In the cities and the towns. On the edges of the busy roads. In the concrete-block shops, shoved in hard between Chinese takeaways and ten-dollar barbers, with drip-tailed white signs painted straight on to the glass —

FRESH FISH. Snapper. Cod. Warehou. Cooked While You Wait! Hot Dogs. Fried Mussels. Family Packs. And on the bricks next to the door and up on the faded awning in permanent letters, red and white — FISH 'n' CHIPS FISH 'n' CHIPS.

A shop with a Formica counter and an old till. One, two, three, four fat fryers behind. Plastic chairs along the wall by the door below a poster, *New Zealand Commercial Fish Species*, and a pile of women's magazines with the titles cut off sitting on the edge of the counter. There's a buzzer that sounds when the door is opened. One, two sharp notes, up and down.

Pale linoleum on the floor that has to be mopped one, two, three, four times a day. Keep everything clean. Keep it all wiped down, spotless. Otherwise they'll close us up faster than you can blink. Don't think they wouldn't. Now come on, girl, here's a customer. Get out there. Hurry up. They haven't got all day.

Owner-operators. Small men, dark-haired men, in blue or white aprons, with permanent squints from standing over the steaming oil. Immigrants and the sons of immigrants who fold paper around the orders quickly without looking down at their hands, one, two, three, four, like origami.

Hurry up, girl! Hurry up!

A permanent frown and a silent shadowy wife. With a distracted daughter of eighteen who wears her black hair back from her head as she serves behind the counter and thinks about romantic old movies and where she'd rather be.

CHORUS

Two fish and a scoop thanks, love. Yeah, two fish and a scoop. Ya well? That's the trick. Been busy? That right? And chuck in a hot dog with that, why don't ya. And you there, hey there, girl, smile, it might not happen. Two fish and a scoop thanks, love. Two fish and a scoop.

VERSE TWO

Yeah, yeah. That's what she's worried about; that it might not happen. Or worse, that it might be happening here and now in her father's shop while she's dressed in a white apron with a grease stain on the front. They order, looking up at the board above and behind her, talking to the empty space near the top of her head. She bangs the basket one, two, on the edge of the fryer and droplets of yellowed oil fall back with a patter. The chips hit the paper with a sudden clatter. The salt goes on, one, two, three, four shakes. There are cars going by outside in a steady stream, the first headlights coming on. She can hear the soft jazz-drum hiss of their tyres on the road.

Four fish, two scoops . . . nah, make that five fish.

Five fish, two scoops?

Yeah. Yeah annnnd . . . nah that'll do.

Five fish, two scoops?

. . . Nah, yeah.

The stoned guys with the red-veined eyes and a craving. The men in white shirts, their ties loose around their necks. The blokes in metal-toed work boots who track mud on the floor. Women with kids on their knees, tired and twitchy. Old men who want to talk about the fish they used to catch, and young girls in dark mascara on their way to awkward parties. They come through the door alone and in pairs, threes and fours. She listens to them talk while she works.

Have you heard?

No, what?

He's left his wife for her!

No. For her?

Yes.
No. For Fleur?

Martin is letting me use his holiday home in
Marlborough.
That's a bit of a coup.
Come up at Christmas. We'd love to see you.
I might just do that.
Do. Do.

You got a buck?
Nah.
Sucks.
I'm outta here.
Yeah.

Things are starting to pick up now as the rush-hour
traffic really begins to flow. The door buzzer goes off
again: buzzes as they come and buzzes as they leave, one,
two, one, two. She's got more baskets on the go. The oil
boils with a steady rhythm.

There's a dagger-nosed woman who nudges her son
forward. Kid must be about three or four. Go on go on you
order, says the mother. Tell the lady what you want. You
said you wanted to, Jason.

Doughnuts and fish, he half whispers, looking down at
the floor where some stray chips have fallen. One, two.

Sorry? I can't hear you.

He said three doughnuts and four fish. And the chips,
she snaps down at the kid. You have to say about the chips.

One chips. Surly now.

The woman squeezes his arm, what looks like hard.

What do you say?

Please.

Don't worry about him, the mother says with a tight smile. He's just having a bad day.

Her father comes out from the back to help, grumbling in Cantonese beneath his breath about how she's vague as a ghost and how low they are on pre-battered fish. If they run out there'll be hell to pay. The door buzzes. The till rings. She tries to concentrate but always seems to be thinking about other things: something she saw in a romantic movie; the lyrics from a song; or whether the new shampoo has really taken the smell of the shop out of her hair.

CHORUS

Two fush and a scoop thanks, love. Twooo fush and a scoop and don't be shy with the chips eh, girl. How's ya day been? Good as gold. Can't complain. Least work's over for the week, again. Two fush and a scoop thanks, sweetheart. Two fush and a scoop.

VERSE THREE

One, two, three, four blokes from the council gang come in. They've been working on the drains, digging up a street nearby. All orange vests and nudging elbows. She catches the eye of the young guy with the dark wavy hair who trails in behind the others. She's seen him before and he gives her half a grin and raises his eyebrows in the workman's salute. Her heart beats louder, one, two, one, two.

Hello.

Gidday.

What would you like?

. . . Fish and a scoop, thanks?

How many?

Two.

His mate, the one with the beer gut way out over his belt, picks up a magazine. Hey, look at this. Tom and Penelope are on the rocks. Says here that she's dating again. Maybe I'll give it a shot.

Peals of laughter in the small space.

As if, Lou . . .

Yeah right . . .!

Hey, yeah, yeah.

Too skinny by half.

True.

Reckon Tracy would have something to say too.

She sees that the young guy with dark wavy hair, like a movie star, has a way of listening with his head cocked to one side. It makes her think that he's hearing something different from everyone else, something between the words that no one else can quite catch.

CHORUS

Two fish and a scoop thanks, love. Yeah, two fish and a scoop. So how do you think the All Blacks will do? Ya reckon? I'll say! And maybe that's true. Keeping busy? Not bad. Not much. Just the same. Bit windy out now. Might rain (or might not). Two fish and a scoop thanks, love. Two fish and a scoop.

VERSE FOUR

And the chips come out as the fish goes in and she bangs the basket on the edge of the fryer, one, two, three, four. And she wonders if the young guy with the dark hair and the small scar on his chin like Harrison Ford will ask her out. Perfect droplets of yellowed oil fall back with a patter. The oil bubbles in a staccato rhythm. She empties the whole lot on to the paper with a sound like a sudden clash of tambourines. The salt goes on, one, two, three, four. And if you squint hard the dripping tails of the signs painted on the glass look like musical notes.

The young guy with the dark wavy hair is drumming his fingers on the edge of his plastic chair. His foot is tapping on the lino. The dark-haired girl behind the counter meets his eye across the crowded room and she says something he doesn't quite catch.

What? Sorry?

Your order.

Oh yeah.

Two fish and a scoop.

Yeah, yeah, that's right, that's mine, thanks, yeah.

The buzzer sounds, one, two, up and down. The customers talk. The till rings. The traffic streams by outside in a steady line and the streetlights flicker and come on, one, two, three, four. Her father bangs the basket on the edge of the fryer. Her guy's footsteps sound on the white linoleum as he stands and walks towards her.

She watches him move like a guy in an old movie pushing through a train station crowd, looking for the woman. And the soundtrack plays loudest in the tense seconds just before he sees her.

And then, at the exact moment when he reaches the counter, a sudden unheralded silence opens up. Everything, even the traffic, stops for a few seconds. And in that gap he takes the warm white packet from her, his fingers softly brushing the back of her hand.

maniototo six

Egg tempura on canvas — 590 x 500 mm

The missing painting is a small landscape of the Maniototo by Grahame Sydney. He admired it immediately for its emotive depiction of the folding ground, the morning shadows creeping across barren hills, yellowed tussock in the foreground. It is the sky, however, which dominates the piece: indescribably huge and empty. A vast expanse of blues fading down to almost white where it doesn't quite connect with the land. Almost, it seems, pushing the earth away, subjugating it, forcing it down so that it occupies less than its fair share of the available space. Sydney has included a slight clue to the season. Fingers of snow seen in the shadowed valleys suggest autumn or early spring, and in the foreground a small patch of unmelted snow lies in the shadow beneath a clump of tussock. It is early morning or possibly late evening. The shadows are long. The light is crisp. There is absolutely nothing, nothing at all romantic about this lighting. This is in no way the buttery light of traditional English romantic pastoralism.

Mark has owned this painting for fifteen years. It was one of the first important works in his private collection. One of the first paintings he truly loved. He bought it from the artist directly. It hung in a recess next to his front door where he could admire it as he came and went or moved between the kitchen and the bedrooms. And now it is gone. It has been stolen from his home. It would not have been a difficult item to steal; to lift it from the wall and conceal it inside a large handbag or beneath a buttoned-up coat would have been a matter of moments. The frame was oak, narrow and very light.

The obvious culprit is his son, Richard.

The previous evening Richard had arrived unexpectedly at Mark's fiftieth birthday party. Of course Richard was invited but Mark had not expected his son to materialise. On the phone Richard had mumbled something about exams, had clearly intimated that he would not be making the trip up from Dunedin.

But arrive he did, and there was a girl with him. They had stood outside on the terrace, not mixing, notably apart from the other guests. Both appeared to smoke constantly. Smoking is not a habit that Mark is comfortable with. His son, as a medical student, a future doctor, should know better.

The girl kept on a long brown overcoat buttoned down the front. Mark's first impression was of a short solid frame

— what in a less correct era men would have openly referred to as child-bearing hips. She was not fat but approaching that condition. Richard himself had on what looked like a second-hand jacket over a pair of jeans, tattered and dangling at the heel. His one concession to propriety was a mismatched tie. He looked tired. Dark creases loitered beneath his eyes and he appeared to have lost weight. There was an unfamiliar gauntness to his face.

Mark had found himself irritated by his son's appearance. Couldn't Richard have made more of an effort? Surely with a bit of forethought it would have been possible to borrow or even buy some more appropriate clothes. After all, the deputy mayor was here as well as several trustees of the gallery. Would a simple haircut have been too much? His son's hair was moppish, frizzled above the ears, and his sideburns were long. It was completely unnecessary to have Richard looking like a refugee among his guests. How long could he be expected to cling to this bohemian image of the down-at-heel student before entering a more mature phase of his life?

'Hello Richard. Are you enjoying yourselves?' They did not embrace or even shake hands. Mark had felt the girl's scrutiny.

'Sarah, this is my father. This is Sarah.'

'It's nice to meet you, Sarah. Please call me Mark.'

'Hello.'

He had wondered what happened to Richard's last girlfriend. A pleasant enough young woman, although he couldn't immediately remember her name. This new girl's hair was too short, cut in a no doubt fashionably jagged bowl but left long at the back, and a natural black that went well with her dark skin. Despite her hairdresser's efforts, however, she was undeniably pretty. Her face was a symmetrical oval, her eyes large. Large dark eyes. He thought of the Tahitian women in Gauguin's later work, posed semi-nude alone and in small groupings. It was a full face, yet it still managed to be strong. A face to match her body.

'When did you get in to town?'

'Yesterday.'

'I hope you didn't miss anything important on your course just for my birthday.'

'I was coming up anyway.'

'I see.' There was an awkward pause. 'Where are you staying?'

'With friends.'

'You know that you're always welcome to stay here. Both of you. I've got room.'

'We're okay. We're staying with friends.'

Perhaps it was just as well. No doubt there would be stresses involved if Richard and this girl, Sarah, if they stayed in his home. His offer had been made. The girl turned her head and watched the other guests as they stood in small groups in front of the paintings. He had taken that as his cue to make the usual excuses and leave.

He had not really noticed them after that. His impression was that they had stayed outside. He was sure that they had not mixed with the other guests. Someone had made a comment later in the evening suggesting that dope was being smoked in the courtyard. He had decided to let sleeping dogs lie. About midnight Richard and the girl had said a perfunctory goodbye and were gone. If anything, he had been relieved.

It was only much later, after all the guests had gone and

he himself had retired to bed, that he noticed the painting
was missing. He had been unable to sleep and had fetched
himself a glass of water. It was while carrying it back to his
room that the painting's absence registered. There is a
nook in the wall close to the front door, filled by a small
oak table where he leaves his keys, the spot where he sorts
his mail. Something had struck him as being not right and
he turned on the single recessed ceiling light to reveal
a slightly darker patch of wall, an empty picture hook near
its apex.

He had stood staring at the empty space until his bare
feet grew cold against the tiles.

Yes, he is sure. There is absolutely no doubt in his mind
that Richard is responsible. The question now is what is he
going to do about it?

Two days later he travels to Dunedin. For the most
part the road south is straight and makes for boring
driving. Occasionally he glimpses the Pacific Ocean on his
left as, south of Timaru, the highway draws in conspira-
torially to follow the coast. Apart from the heavy trucks
there is little traffic midweek. By habit he drives
cautiously, and the trucks overtake him in the passing
lanes, their drivers staring down at him from the high cabs
as his car shudders in their turbulence.

Within five hours of leaving his house he is entering
Dunedin. The highway ascends a steep hill and he has his
first glimpse of the city wrapping itself around the head
of the narrow harbour like a patterned shawl of white and
red roofs.

He has booked a room at a motel on George Street,
close to the centre of the city. The pug-faced Asian woman
at reception walks him across the concrete courtyard to his

room with its faded pastels, blue and pink. She points out where the tea bags are kept and hands him a small green carton of milk for the morning. Then she leaves him alone. He is not anticipating that his business with Richard will require him to stay here more than one night. Of course he has tried to call, but his son's number is no longer in service. Nor is his cellphone. Consequently Richard is not expecting him. Probably it is just as well.

The address he has turns out to be a squat weatherboard house on the hills close to the green belt, up by the public swimming pool. It reminds him in some ways of his father's old home on the hills which was sold three years ago after his father succumbed to a brain tumour. He parks his car on the narrow street, pulling the handbrake on hard, and angles the wheels in towards the gutter. The house is surrounded by a dense, seemingly unplanned garden of native trees, the path overgrown with five-finger and ragged pittosporum. There is a clearing close to the house, a patch of weeds he thinks must once have been a lawn. Near its centre charcoaled planks of wood and half-burnt faggots of newspaper lie in a rain-sodden pile.

The door is answered by a girl of no more than eighteen whose hair is dyed a violent shade of red. Small sleepy eyes, marsupial eyes, he thinks, question his presence.

'I'm looking for Richard. Richard Alymer.'

'I think you've got the wrong house.'

'I was given this address.' For lack of anything else to do, he hands over the piece of paper he is holding.

She frowns, barely glancing at it, and half-shrugs and begins to back away.

'Could you please ask if anyone else knows him.'

She looks doubtful but says 'Okay,' and turns and

retreats into the dim interior of the house. He waits on the porch where he hears a surge of noise from a television set as an internal door is opened. There are muted voices under the soundtrack for an advertisement for batteries. Are these people students like Richard? Don't they have lectures to go to? Even if they are not students, there must be better things to do in the middle of the day than sit in front of a television.

The girl returns. 'Nick thinks there was a guy called Richard here before we moved in. No one knows where he's at now.'

'He didn't leave a forwarding address? A phone number?'

She is already shaking her head and has closed the door before he has finished talking. She has taken his piece of paper with her, and he is left standing on the porch, clutching nothing more substantial than an uncollaborated rumour of his son.

But he is reluctant to give up so easily. It is not in his nature to leave without thoroughly exploring every possibility. He drives back into town and parks as close to the campus as he can. From there he walks. The original gothic buildings are now cheek by jowl with concrete towers from the 1970s and more recent glass-faced lecture theatres. It is, he thinks, an aesthetic mess.

At the student registry he explains that he has paid a surprise visit on his son but has somehow foolishly managed to lose the boy's address. No, there is no one at home at the moment whom he can call to find out the information. The woman behind the information desk must be in her sixties but has pale copper streaks in her hair. He wonders if the streaks are an attempt to blend in, to give

herself that air of youthful experimentation that he has
observed in the students he has seen around campus.

'I was wondering if you had my son's new address in
your records.'

'I can check.'

She turns back to her computer screen. He is surprised
it is that easy, that she is willing to part with a student's
personal information so informally. She has not even taken
the precaution of asking for identification. Her fingers tap
the keyboard and there is a pause. He watches her reading
from the screen.

'I'm sorry but our records show that Richard Alymer is
no longer enrolled.'

'There must be some mistake. He's doing fourth-year
medical. Could you check again please?'

'Richard Edward Alymer?' She gives Richard's date
of birth, her finger now tracing the screen in front of her
as though the information is written there in Braille.

'Yes. That's right.'

'The only records we have for him are from the last
academic year. He didn't complete his course and hasn't
re-enrolled this year.'

'I see. And you have no address?'

'The last address we have is Willis Street. Is that any
good.'

'No. That's out of date.'

He thanks her for her help and walks out into the
sunlight. So Richard has dropped out of university, has
given up his medical studies. There is no mistake. For six
months — no, for longer, for a portion of last year as well
— Richard has been telling him blatant lies. His son has
been concocting a life of lectures and exams while actually

. . . He is unable to complete the sentence. What has Richard been doing? He has no idea. His son's activities over the preceding months are a complete mystery to him.

He hears no bell, but suddenly doors are flung open and students spill out into the sunlight in colourful groups. They chatter, laughing loudly. The end of lectures. He is struck by how very young they look, how fresh faced and optimistic. They fill the paths in course streams. He is standing still in the middle of a path, unsure where to go and what to do now. He finds himself in their way. He is unexpectedly surrounded and facing against the current. A girl bumps his arm with her tasselled shoulder-bag but does not apologise. Young people sidestep, flood around him and past. Out of desperation he moves from the path on to the lawn and watches them go by.

He had intended to go running during his time here. Now, at a loss for what else to do, what to think, he drives back to his hotel and gets changed.

Running is something he has taken up only in the last few years. Since his father's death really. He freely acknowledges that it was the spectre of ill health that made him seriously consider his own well-being. He runs three or four times a week, mostly in the park in the early evenings when it is still light. Sometimes he meets up with Martin, a colleague from the gallery, but mostly he runs alone. There can be no doubt he feels better for it and has lost some weight around his middle. Not that jogging is any protection against the type of thing that killed his father. Brain tumours, he knows, are more random but at least he can be said to be proactive, to be battling the more avoidable conditions that afflict men of his age.

But he is not used to running on hills. He discovers that

a different rhythm is required: something slower than his usual pace, relying more on leg power. He runs slowly past rows of solid brick houses, two and even three storeyed and obviously expensive, but closer to the road than they would be in a city with more room to sprawl. He is unsure of his route. Twice he heads up a cul-de-sac and is forced to turn and retrace his steps. Other streets end in long rows of concrete steps that snake-and-ladder him up to the next level of streets. He stops more often than he would in the park.

By the time he gets to the green belt he is breathing hard. A wide band of bush has been preserved on the hills above the centre of the city. From streets of suburban houses he suddenly finds himself on a stretch of road surrounded by tall trees that arch overhead. The transition is almost instantaneous. There are houses and then . . . this. It is like moving from the open into a moist cave. The light is mottled. There are ferns growing on the earth banks next to the footpath. The road no longer climbs but is almost level, traversing the bowl of the hills. He is now running parallel with the narrow harbour, which he glimpses occasionally through breaks in the bush.

For him one of the appeals of running is that while he is moving he does not have to think. It is pure doing. But today his mind slips repeatedly, annoyingly, back to Richard. Richard has stolen from him. Now it appears he has also dropped out of university. He has been hiding behind a well-constructed wall of lies. Mark is at a loss to explain any of Richard's actions. He has to accept the fact that his son is a stranger to him.

Ahead of him a group of women round a corner. There are seven or eight and they are walking briskly, swinging their arms like foppish soldiers. No doubt some type of walking group for women warding off the spread of hips and thighs. It is only when he gets closer that he sees that all of them are pregnant. They approach him in a ragged echelon, their bellies riding out in front. Most of the women walk with a look of dogged determination, as though the well-being of their unborn children depends on the vigour with which they perform this exercise.

As he passes, a blonde woman on the outside edge of the group makes eye contact. She has a wide, open face that he immediately likes. Her belly is covered by a bright white T-shirt several sizes too large' for her. The writing on the shirt says, BABY ON BOARD! She smiles at him, acknowledging the absurdity of her situation. He smiles back. For a passing moment they are co-conspirators. And then his eyes flick forward and his legs have carried him past.

He runs for an hour. The road through the green belt loops around, leading him back into suburban streets. He moves downhill, walking on the steeper stretches to preserve his sometimes fragile knees, until he is back on George Street close to the Octagon. He is almost back to his motel when he sees the girl, Richard's partner from the party. She is walking in the same direction as him but on the other side of the street. There is no mistaking her. He recognises the short black hair, the rounded soft features. She is even wearing the same overcoat she wore the other night.

He crosses the street and slips in behind her, keeping back amongst the crowd of students who clutter the footpath between them. He feels absurd moving in furtive spurts like this, loitering in shop entrances, a figure straight out of the movies. He considers catching up, confronting her and demanding to know where Richard is. It is possible that he could bully her into taking him to his son. He is just about to catch her up when she turns and enters a pawn shop. Is Richard using her to canvass potential buyers for the Sydney? He doubts that she has the painting with her. Richard is not that stupid (he cannot speak for the girl). Only a stupid person would walk the streets trying to hawk something as immediately recognisable as a stolen painting. Unless they are counting on him not having reported the theft. An assumption which in the event has proved correct.

He walks past the shop and waits in a doorway where comic books are on display. After a few minutes the girl appears again and continues walking. He turns and pretends to be examining a rare early edition of the *Green Lantern*, and then when she is past he follows her. She walks until the shops thin out and give way to rows of tidy but plain wooden houses. She turns down a side street and then another. There are fewer people on the footpaths here, and he slows his pace, dropping back further. If she glances back he is sure she will recognise him immediately. He is poised to turn suddenly into a stranger's driveway or dart up a garden path.

Clouds have blown in from the south in a dirty smear. Now it starts to rain, drizzle which drifts down from a low concrete sky. He is still wearing only his T-shirt and shorts and is suddenly freezing. He should have thought to bring a windbreaker. He can feel the first drops of rain against the skin of his arms and at the back of his neck. Up ahead of him the girl puts her head down and begins to walk faster.

The well-maintained homes have given way to rental accommodation, large houses which he imagines have been divided into as many bedrooms as possible. They present sagging fences and unpainted walls to the street. Nearly every one seems to have a battered couch gracing the veranda. The girl walks doggedly on until she abruptly turns in. He picks up his pace.

A wooden gate, part of a tall concrete-block fence. Number 27. He looks around for a sign showing the name of the street but cannot see one. Red and yellow circulars have spilt from the letterbox and litter the footpath. He slips his hand in through the arched hole in the gate, fumbles for the latch and lifts it. The gate has sagged on its hinges and scrapes along the concrete path as he pushes it open. He waits but there is no response to the noise.

Inside the property there is an overgrown lawn. He follows the path up to the front of the bungalow and knocks on the door.

A pause. 'Who is it?' The girl's voice. She is clearly wary.

'Mark Alymer. Richard's father.'

There is a pause long enough to make him think she has retreated back into the depths of the house, but then he hears a key turn and the door is opened. She is shorter than he remembers and obviously scared. She is looking him up and down, obviously curious about his clothing.

'Richard isn't here.'

'It's Sarah, isn't it? You came to my house the other night.'

'Yes.'

'Can you tell me when he's going to be back?'

She shakes her head. 'I don't know. He didn't tell me.'

For all he knows Richard is inside the house at this very moment, perhaps even listening as they speak. Mark has not come to Dunedin to play childish games of hide-and-seek with his son. The girl still remains half behind the door, revealing only her face.

'Tell him that I am looking for him. That I have come especially to talk to him. There is something very important that we have to discuss. He'll know what I'm talking about.'

If the girl knows about the painting, she gives no indication. Her face remains impassive. 'Okay. I'll tell him.'

'I'm staying at the Ambassador Motel. Do you have a pen and paper?'

'I know where it is.'

'On George Street. I'll write my cellphone number down. In case Richard has lost it. Do you have a pen and paper?'

She frowns. 'Wait a minute.'

She returns a few minutes later with a small rectangle of white paper and a ballpoint pen which he has to shake hard before the ink flows. He writes the address and phone number down, aware of the girl watching him. She is never still, shifting her weight, moving her stockinged feet. He writes CALL ME in block capitals and circles the words several times, and then hands her back the paper and the pen.

'Will you make sure he gets it. It's very important that he calls me today.'

'Okay. I'll tell him.'

She is about to close the door. He reaches out and puts his hand lightly against the wood. 'Sarah, can you tell me, is Richard in some type of trouble?'

She drops her eyes and shakes her head with a rattling motion like a dog with a stick. 'If Richard thought I was talking to you he'd be really angry. I'll give him your message though.'

She closes the door and he is left standing on the veranda. So Richard is not inside. The rain is falling harder now, and the wind from off the harbour has picked up. It is only as he is leaving the property that he thinks how he must look in his shorts and sodden T-shirt, water dripping from his nose. Closing the gate behind him, he sets off back towards the motel, moving at a slow jog in a futile attempt to keep warm.

Richard has not called.

Mark sits on the couch in his motel room with the work he has brought with him spread across the glass coffee table. It is just after ten o'clock and the hard rain strikes the roof, filling the room with a white noise that almost drowns out the soft hiss of the cars driving by on George Street.

He is just about to retire to bed when there is a knock on the door. He opens it, expecting to see Richard or the pug-faced manager with a message, but instead it is the girl again, Sarah. Her short hair is wet, slicked down across her scalp. Rainwater drips from the cuffs of her jacket. There is another change from when he saw her this afternoon. An ugly bruise hangs over her left eye, lumped and dark. The eye itself is bloodshot. She stands dripping, edgy, undecided; looks back towards the street.

'I need to talk to you.'

'Come in.'

He steps aside to let her pass and watches as she crosses the room. She removes her overcoat and drapes it,

sodden, across the back of the couch. It is the first time he
has seen her without it. When she turns to face him it is
immediately apparent that she is pregnant. She is wearing
dark leggings under a long woollen dress, the hem of which
is darkly wet where it hung down below the coat. The
dress moulds to the curve of her hips and thighs, revealing
the unmistakable arc of her belly. Of course. He should
have picked it before.

So this explains the overcoat. Richard did not want
him to know.

She picks up the proofs of the gallery newsletter, and
he watches her leaf through the pages. 'What is this?'

He gently takes them from her. 'Is there something you
want?'

She blinks and looks around the room. 'I need to talk
to you about Richard.' She draws in her breath and speaks
without looking at him. 'I'm pregnant. Richard is the
father.'

As if to prove his son's paternity she uses her hands to
further flatten the material across her belly. He can clearly
see the full curve of her now, and guesses that she is about
halfway through her term — twenty, maybe as many as
twenty-five weeks. It is hard to be precise. It has been a
long time since he has been called upon to judge the extent
of a woman's pregnancy. Too far along though, certainly, to
arrange for an abortion.

So here is his explanation for Richard's behaviour. This
young woman, in what his own mother would have called
a *delicate condition*. This is undoubtedly the cause of
Richard's distraction, his life-crisis, the reason for the
abandonment of his studies. Possibly this is also the reason
he saw fit to take the Sydney. Mark is, if anything, relieved

to discover that his son is suffering from such a traditional malady.

She is watching him closely, gauging his reaction.

'I hope you won't be insulted if I ask whether you are sure that Richard is the father?'

She takes no offence (which in itself makes him believe there may be some doubt). 'Richard knows that it's his. He'll tell you.'

'I see. And when is this baby due?'

She has to think. 'I'm about six months now. It's due in August. I saw a nurse at Family Planning. She told me I was pregnant. I thought I might be, but she told me that I was.'

It is clear to him that she has made some effort for this meeting, that this has been thought through. He sees now that she has tried to camouflage the bruise around her eye with makeup. There is lipstick and eyeliner in relatively modest amounts by student standards. He detects perfume. This dress is probably her best.

'Why have you chosen to tell me now after you both went to so much trouble to keep me in the dark?'

'Richard's kicked me out. Out of the flat.'

'I saw you there this afternoon.'

'We had a fight when he came back. He threw most of my stuff out the window. I didn't have anywhere to put it, so I just left it on the veranda out of the rain.' The thought of her evicted possessions seems to make her forlorn and she sits on the arm of the couch and hangs her head.

'Were you fighting about the painting you stole from my house?'

He waits for her to deny responsibility, but to her credit she nods. It is a quick, almost involuntary gesture.

'I told him you might help us if we gave it back. He took the painting to a guy he knows but he was only going to give him a hundred dollars for it.' She touches her stomach again with the flat of her hand, moving it in the circular rubbing motion he thinks of as common to all pregnant women.

'So what is it you want from me?'

'We'll need money for the baby. For food and stuff.'

'You have just admitted that you stole from me. Why would I be at all inclined to give you money?'

'You're Richard's father.'

'Richard is an adult. He is old enough to deal with his own problems, with this . . . situation.' He cannot think of a better expression. 'He has made his own bed. It's no longer my place to take care of my son or his child, either financially or in any other way. And frankly I don't think Richard would thank me if I did interfere.'

He watches as she tucks her head like a bird, burrowing her chin into her shoulder, and starts to cry. But he is not going to let himself be manipulated.

'You must have friends, family. People you can ask for help?'

She shakes her head. 'Both my parents are dead. I have a brother in Scotland but we don't get on. He won't want to know about it.'

He persists. 'But you must have friends here in Dunedin. Somewhere you can go.'

She shakes her head again and will not be drawn by further questions about her family. It occurs to him that he could be the intended victim of an elaborate confidence trick. Really, he knows nothing about this girl. It may be that she has taken advantage of her pregnancy to collect money, gifts, free board, who knows what else, in this manner before. Possibly she has convinced other men that she is carrying their child, their grandchild.

'Stop crying. I can't talk to you properly when you're crying.'

He crosses to the window and shifts the heavy curtain with his hand so that he can see out. It is still raining. The drops hit the sill in the light spilling from the room. If anything it is raining harder than before.

'I need to talk to Richard. Tonight. Do you know where he is now?'

'Yes.'

'Will you take me to him?'

She nods.

The girl directs him back to the flat. She sits next to him, bleary eyed and silent, as the windscreen wipers shift the water across the glass. A dozen cars are now parked in front of the house, and water is pooled, inching across the road where the drain is clogged with the spilled advertising from the letterbox. She fumbles for the latch on the gate and he follows her through.

There is a party in progress. The house emits a steady bass thump. Despite the cold, several windows are open and squares of pale red light spill on to the grass. Shadowy figures loiter on the porch, drinking from cans and bottles. The girl moves quickly past him and vanishes through the open doorway into the crowded hall. Mark hesitates, unwilling to fully commit himself to this house, to this crush of people. It is in all likelihood the wrong time to be confronting his son. But if not now, then when?

There is a pile of jumbled possessions stacked on the open porch by the door. It at least partially confirms the girl's story of hasty eviction. He identifies a torn duvet, clothing, a desk drawer stacked with tapes and compact disks, a stuffed toy giraffe. Several people stare at him curiously. They yell at each other above the music.

Inside there is a strong smell of beer and marijuana. There are even more people than he first thought. The house is bulging at the seams. Someone has painted all the light bulbs red. He glances into rooms and sees by the Martian light people standing, leaning against walls, splayed over beds and sofas, sprawled across the floor. Several seem to be sleeping or unconscious. People sway to the bass rhythm. Couples openly kiss and fondle each other. But there is no sign of Richard.

In the kitchen, dishes caked with dried food sit in piles in the sink and spread across the bench where someone has spilt brown sugar. Two more bags of sugar sit on the Formica table among a litter of unopened mail and more dishes. Among the smells, he can now distinguish the rubbish bag gaping open in the corner. A group of people sit around the kitchen table. A red-headed woman in a thick jersey slumps forward into her arms. No one speaks to him and the woman does not move at all.

Richard suddenly appears. He is wearing faded jeans and a sweatshirt with an old-fashioned V collar that shows the dark hair on his chest. His shoulders are coat-hangers on which the sweatshirt hangs, barely touching his body.

'Hi.'

'Hello, Richard.'

As he watches, Richard crosses to the bench and fills the jug awkwardly, barely able to fit it beneath the tap. He is obviously slightly drunk or stoned. 'You should've given me a bit of warning before you called around, eh. The place is a bit of a mess at the moment. We're having a bit of a party to celebrate.'

To celebrate what? he wonders. Richard does not elaborate and he does not ask.

It infuriates him that Richard should act as though there is nothing at all amiss between them, as though he has just dropped by for a cup of tea. They both know this is not simply an unexpected social call. The girl slumped over the table still has not moved. The others have gone back to their own conversation.

'Richard, I've been trying to get hold of you.'

'Haven't you got my new number? I thought I'd given it to you. I've been busy, you know. There's exams all the way through the year. I've got to study a lot to keep on top of it all.'

So many untruths in the space of one utterance. 'Don't lie to me any more, Richard. I've spoken to the university. I know you've dropped out. You haven't even been enrolled this year.'

If he had expected denials, shouting, histrionics, then he is disappointed. Richard is po-faced, silent.

'Why didn't you tell me if you were having trouble with the course? We could have talked about the situation, maybe arranged something with the university, some type of break.'

'I didn't need to talk to you. It was my decision to leave. That's it, end of story.'

'So you're just going to waste three years of study and leave yourself with no direction, no future.'

'Obviously I think I have a future. It's you who think dropping out of bloody university is the end of my life.'

'That's not what I said.'

'I don't even see why we are discussing this. It's my decision.'

Richard is at least partially right. He is old enough to make his own decisions and, by extension, to have to live with the consequences. As a father, Mark cannot be expected to police his son's life. If this is the path Richard has chosen to stumble along, then so be it.

'All right, I agree. We won't discuss your leaving university any further. I didn't come here to talk about that. When you were at my home recently I have reason to believe you took a painting. It is a painting of which I am particularly fond and I have come to get it back from you.'

'Okay.'

In the end it is as simple as that. Okay. Richard turns and walks from the room.

Mark follows him through the crowded hallway into a small room, a deserted laundry, at the back of the house. There is no washing machine, but the plumbing for one protrudes from the floor. Mark watches as Richard uses a key to open a cupboard in the corner and takes out the Sydney. It is wrapped in newspaper tied together with binding twine. Richard hands it to him, and he unwraps it. He is relieved to see that the painting is undamaged.

'Aren't you at least going to apologise?'

Richard shrugs thin shoulders. 'You've got it back now.'

'If you'd been anyone else I would have called the police days ago. I hope you appreciate that.'

'I took your precious painting, okay. I tried to sell it for money but I couldn't. You've got it back now. Why don't you just go?'

He is suddenly furious. 'Do you seriously think you can just dismiss me? That I'm going to leave it at that.

Richard, you stole from me. Do you have any idea how seriously I treat that?'

'Call the police then. Go on.'

'I should.'

'Go on, the phone's in the hall. Call them!' Richard is waving his hands agitatedly in the air.

Who is this doppelgänger, this haggard parody of his son?

'I want you to acknowledge that what you did was a gross betrayal.'

'I don't need a lecture!'

'Frankly, Richard, I don't know what you need.'

'Fuck off! Just leave me alone!'

'Right. I'm going to leave now.'

'Go on then, fucking leave!' And Richard snatches something from the cupboard shelf and, bending back his arm, throws it towards him in a short whiplash. It hits him in the chest. He feels it as a dull thump like an ill-timed heartbeat.

Mark looks down to see a glass paperweight fall to the ground. Inside is swirling snow, a Christmas scene. It hits the floorboards near his foot and rolls away. Without any conscious thought, he crosses the space between himself and his son. He has Richard by the top of the arms and is shaking him hard. His son's arms feel bony, the muscles wasted beneath his palms.

Then Richard punches him. It is a swinging uppercut that only partially connects with his jaw. He feels his son's knuckles graze across his cheek, and then he is striking back. It is a reflex action. He feels his fist connect with Richard's face, the nose gristling sideways into the cheek a fraction of a second before the solidity of the teeth, the bone against his knuckles. There is a sharp pain in his hand and he realises that he may have broken his own thumb. And then Richard is falling back. Is lying on the floor looking up with blood already flowing down his face. Is reaching out his hands to ward off another blow.

Before Mark can react, hit him again or take him in his arms, strong hands are dragging him away. There is a swirl of angry faces as Mark is manhandled out of the room and down the corridor. The music is still playing. People are shouting. He is shouting. He looks desperately for Sarah but cannot see her. He falls and for a moment has a close-up view of a woman's shoe. There are small hand-painted flowers on the leather strap. Someone kicks him hard in the thigh and his leg goes instantly numb. And then he is pulled to his feet again, dragged and shoved, and with a final lurch is propelled out from the porch and on to the muddy lawn.

He falls and somehow manages to get back to his feet. Turning back to the house, he sees a wall of angry faces. Richard is not among them. Someone throws a full beer can and it brushes his arm before hitting the fence with a solid thump. Turning, he limps to the gate and out on to the street where his car is parked.

Sarah catches up to him as he is opening the door. 'Wait.' She thrusts the painting towards him. Newspaper hangs loosely from it. She is clearly in a panic. 'Take it. Please. Richard's sorry that he took it.'

'He's not sorry at all,' he says angrily.

She glances back through the open gate towards the house. 'I shouldn't tell you, but he owes money to some people. That's why he took it, because he needed the money to pay them back.'

So, he thinks, it is back to money again, seemingly the

theme of all his conversations with this girl. 'Richard is very lucky that I haven't pressed charges against him, against you both. I'm going now.'

'What about me? What about the baby?'

'Not my responsibility.'

She has the sudden look of a poor swimmer who finds she is out of her depth. He gets into the car and starts the engine. She taps on the glass and he lowers the window reluctantly.

'I've got nowhere to go.'

He considers simply pulling away, leaving her standing on the footpath in the rain. Against his better judgement he reaches over and unlocks the passenger door.

'You can stay for just one night.'

She climbs in next to him without a word, and closes the door.

As he pulls away he glances in through the open gate and sees Richard standing on the front step, looking towards him with an unreadable expression. He drives on.

He folds out the couch into a bed and shows her where the bathroom is. He rings reception and asks for a toothbrush, extra soap and a flannel. The manager sounds annoyed but agrees to bring them.

While they wait he gives her his towel and watches as she lies curled on the bed, drying her hair, rubbing it vigorously with both hands. She is younger than he first thought. Twenty-one, maybe twenty-two is his guess. And now affixed to his son, to him, through this child she is carrying.

'Do you mind if I watch television?' she asks.

'Not if you keep the sound down.'

Without uncurling her body she uses the remote control to flick through the channels. Seemingly at random she selects the end of what looks like a movie from the '60s. He thinks of her not as a cat — which is the obvious metaphor. There is something too stolid about her for a feline comparison. He struggles to find something suitable but is stumped.

In the bathroom he checks his face in the mirror. The left side of his cheek is red and slightly swollen and there is a small cut across his cheek. There is also an angry bruise the size of an orange on his thigh and his thumb is throbbing. He uses a warm flannel to dab at his face. Still, it could have been worse. Richard could have timed his punch better, possibly even shattered his jaw.

There is a knock on the front door. The manager's eyes flick past him as she hands the items over. The girl is still lying curled on the corner of the folded-out bed. He is aware of how it looks.

'My niece has decided to stay with me tonight. There's been a problem at home.'

It is a lie that he immediately regrets. How many nieces has this woman seen sashaying past her office? Young relatives who visit for an hour or two and then slip away. He takes the items, thanks her and closes the door.

'Here you are. I'm going to bed. Good night.'

'Good night.'

'Sarah. I must ask you. Was it Richard who hit you? Did he do that to your face?'

She looks up at him from her place on the bed. 'No, it wasn't Richard. It was someone else.'

But he can tell that she is lying.

He cannot sleep. He lies on his back in the dark for a

long time, staring up at the dimpled ceiling. He can hear the faint sound of the television from the other room and then it is turned off. Finally he leaves his bed to get himself a glass of water from the kitchen tap.

Sarah is in the bathroom. The lounge lights are off but a bright fluorescent glare from the string of small lights above the mirror spills out across the carpet. She has left the bathroom door open, deliberately or not he does not know. He moves past the edge of the bed towards the kitchen and feels as if he is intruding.

In the large mirror he has a clear view of her. She has showered and is standing naked beneath the bright bathroom lights, drying herself with a white towel. She bends towards him from the waist to dab at the moisture on her thighs. She straightens up and begins to rub her short hair.

If she is aware of him in the lounge, she gives no indication.

Her breasts are heavy and he can clearly see the blue veins running down to her nipples which are bruised the same colour as the skin above her eye. He is aware of the dark cross-thatch of hair beneath her swollen stomach where, what is most likely, his first grandchild is hanging between nothingness and life. He looks away.

He returns to his room without the water. Closing the door, he stands with his back against it. His heart is racing as though he has just returned from a run. He wonders what the future will bring. What will become of Richard? And of the girl and this new child, this grandchild? On the chair next to his bed lies the painting, but he takes no solace from its presence.

weight

He stretched his muscles in the sharp light thrown by the naked bulb. It hung above the back door, next to the place where the wood was soft and rotten, but attracted no moths because it was August and the nights were as still and cold as metal. The light barely reached him where he stood in the middle of the lawn, spilling only thinly over his shoulders and back and then stopping, as if exhausted. It carried no warmth, and beyond him there were only shadows.

Stretching forward, he pushed both hands against the raised bark of the old pear tree which pricked into his palms. The tree was old and its roots lifted up the grass beneath his feet. As he stretched he thought about how he would have to get around to taking the whole thing out, borrow the chainsaw from his brother. This year the tree had given only a few pears and even those were small and bitter. Every year there was more fungus and disease on the leaves.

His left leg pushed back and locked so that he felt the muscles of his calf and behind his knee pull tight. He carried little fat, not even around his gut. The tendons on his leg stood out in the cross-light like reinforcing beneath the skin. Changing position, he grasped his ankle with one hand and pulled the leg up behind him. He grunted and felt the tight stretch in his quad. The distant single bulb and the heavy shadows made it look as though the leg had been amputated at the knee.

He heard the sound of the door closing, and his son came out and walked with loping strides over to where his father was standing. They both wore thick sweatshirts and black rugby shorts and running shoes without socks. His son did not speak but stood, his legs wide apart, and slowly circled his head, dipping his chin down to his chest and then opening up his throat to the night sky. The night was perfectly clear, although he could not see many stars because of the reflected light of the city. The son's breath clouded white in front of his face, and his father knew that in the morning there would be a frost on the grass.

'I'd say she's gunna be a cold one,' he said.

'Yeah.' His son began running on the spot, his legs making long shadows that jerked wildly across the grass.

'Probably a frost. It hasn't been bad this year though, milder than usual.'

There was only the faint thud of the son's shoes on the grass. He was eighteen and still mad about what had been said over dinner. He felt that he was old enough now to disagree with his father without being told he was talking back. He had decided that next year he would go flatting, leave home for good.

His father changed position, bending sideways from

the waist, pushing down with his hand towards his bare ankle. 'How was training?'

His son waited before replying. 'Mr Newton is talking about trying me out at lock. Says I'm getting too big to stay at flanker.'

'What does big matter? You're still fast.'

'Yeah, but no one else is as tall. We need someone tall at lock.'

The father grunted. He twisted his body to the left, his hands on his hips. He held himself there and then swung to the right before relaxing into a gentle up down up down rhythm that nearly matched his son's, his toes never leaving the grass. They moved together almost in unison for a few minutes but did not speak.

'Want to get started?' said the father.

'Yeah. Okay.'

The son was the first to the garage door. He grasped the handle and, even though the rollers were rusted and stiff, pulled it up in one movement so that the door lifted into the ceiling space. The light was off and he found the switch and flicked it on. It was a double garage but there was no car, only an expanse of uncracked concrete, smooth and pale like dirty ice. Tools hung from the walls on nails next to a figure-eight of old rope. The smell of weed spray and motor-oil lingered and mixed with the petrol from the cracked tank of the lawnmower.

The son pulled the bench press over beneath the light. Going back, he fetched the dumb-bells, rolling them ahead of him with his foot. He unhooked the weight belt from its nail. It was thick black leather, worn smooth by use so that the white letters had faded away to nothing but faint lines and circles.

His father picked up the bar and laid it across the stand at the head of the bench. He then bent at the knees and picked up the iron plates and slipped them on to the end of the bar. 'You go first.'

'Okay.' He did not look at his father.

He lay back on the bench and pushed himself with his legs so that he slid along until his head was beneath the bar. Reaching up, he measured the distance from the edge so that when he lifted it the bar would be even and balanced. One and a half hand-widths and then his fingers curled. The metal was snow-melt cold. His father stood behind him, ready to lift the weight off should his son fail, although he knew that he would not be needed yet. His son lowered the bar to his chest, pulling in air, and letting the metal gently tap the hollow where his breast bone spread his ribs.

'That's good. Nice and easy. Remember to breathe.' His father's voice came from above and behind. Sixty pounds was not heavy. The son could feel the muscles in his chest and shoulders, cold with the first few repetitions, stretch and warm as the blood pumped into them.

His father had taught him to breathe when he was twelve. He remembered being taken out to the garage after dinner for the first time. His father had pulled the dusty weights from the corner.

'Lie back. No, put your feet down on either side of the bench. That's good.' His father had placed his callused hand on the boy's ribs. There had been no weight on the bar.

'Breathe out on the way down. Never hold your breath.'

His father's fingers had spanned the boy's chest. Heat

had radiated from his palm and seemed to soak downwards. Thinking back now, the son remembered that it was summer and that the sunlight, which seemed to go on late into the night, had leaked through the perspex skylight above him.

'Suck the air in on the way down. Slower. That's right. Breathe. Good, now let it out as you push up.' His father's hand had not been heavy. He remembered feeling disappointed when it was taken away.

Now it was winter and cold, and it was his father's turn. The son gave him the belt and he notched it tightly around his waist. The father lifted more slowly than his son, his eyes fixed on the shadows above him, forehead creased in concentration. He did fifteen repetitions and was breathing hard when he dropped the bar back into its cradle.

Taking a side each, they loaded on more round metal plates. Removing the thin 30s, they slid on a 45 each and then a 20, one on each side, to make it 130 pounds. The plates clinked against each other with a clear note like a brass bell that was cut short as they were pressed together.

The son slid into position, feeling the warmth of his father's body lingering in the bench's padding. He lowered the bar easily to his chest and lifted it, falling into an easy familiar rhythm. His father did not have to help for the final two as he had sometimes done in the past, and the bar rattled back into its cradle.

'So how do you feel about being a lock?'

'It's okay, I s'pose.'

'A lot of locks are wearing headgear these days, even at your level. Stops them getting cauliflower ears.'

'Yeah.'

'I'd still like to see you play at flanker though. Perhaps next year when you move to the club.'

'Okay. Maybe.'

But the son doubted that next year he would be playing for his father's old club. There had been talk of going to Europe. There was also a woman his father did not know about. She did not like him playing in the forwards — playing rugby, full stop.

The father slid on to the bench and grasped the bar. He lowered the weight slowly. He still felt cold, though he had stretched, even after the first set. His muscles felt short and tight. The 130 pounds rose and fell but there was a twinge in his shoulder. His breath huffed out of him, pushed up with the iron weight towards the ceiling. When he had finished the ten repetitions, the same as his son, he sat up and turned so that he was sitting sideways on the bench, his elbows on his knees. There was sweat beneath his hair but he still did not feel warm.

His son slipped off his sweatshirt and hung it on a nail on the wall. He was wearing an old T-shirt, almost too small for him now, and his father saw how the light cast shadows under the curve of his chest and along the ridges at the back of his arms. In a few years he had gone from being tall and skinny to simply big. Solid and still growing.

'I'm feeling good tonight. I'd like to go for it.'

The father stood up. 'Why not?' He smiled but his face felt as tight as his chest.

His son brought the weights that they did not normally use from the corner. Another pair of 45s, a different make, smaller and fatter but still with the large centre holes that let them slip on to the bar. Loading the plates on, working one side each, they bent at the knees and took off the 20s and picked up the 45s and slipped them on next to the first two plates. They worked together so that the bar was never unbalanced and would not flick up and crash down on to the concrete. One hundred and eighty pounds. The son retrieved the 20s from where they sat and, on a whim, slipped them back on.

His father frowned. 'That's two-twenty. You sure you're okay with that?'

'Yeah, I'm feeling good. I'll just try and do one or two.'

'Okay.'

He helped his son lift the bar off its stand, keeping his hands wrapped around it until he was totally sure that the boy had it under control. 'Ready?'

'Yeah.'

The father took his hands away and his son was left holding the whole weight above his body, elbows locked, taking the strain. The boy's arms trembled slightly, and then he bent his elbows and began to lower the weight. He lowered it slowly, sucking in the cold air. The weight barely touched his chest before he was pushing it up and away, keeping it moving. His breath hissed out through his teeth like steam.

'Good. That's one. Doing well.' His father hovered his hands under the bar. He was ready to snatch it up and away when his son's strength was exhausted and the weight threatened to fall back. But his son lowered the bar again and then pushed it slowly back up, wobbling it only slightly as his elbows locked.

'Good, keep breathing.'

And then again. Down and slowly up as though he were pushing away a whole world.

'Okay, that's three. Well done.'

But his son shook his head. 'One more.' His voice was a creak. He sucked in more air and then the bar travelled down. It paused over the chest and then began to inch back up.

'Come on, breathe. You can do it. Lift!'

Slowly the weight was pushed up. The boy's father curled his fingers around the bar, ready to lift it when his son couldn't. But he was not needed. The son's chest was taut and straining, the muscles contracting and bunched. He heard his son's breathing and felt the breath push up against his own face. He smelt the sweet strain of the weight.

And then the weight was at the top of its arc and his father was guiding the bar back into its cradle, rattling and clanging. The son sat up. He breathed in long drags. His expression was triumphant.

'Well, done. That's a lot of weight.' The father stood a little apart and looked at his son.

The boy had never lifted more than him. It had always been natural that he should be stronger, his son weaker, but in the past few months they had both been struggling beneath the weight. Both at the edge of their strength. His muscles ached for days afterwards. Lately, he had found himself making half-recognised excuses not to come out to the garage in the evenings. But never before had either of them had all the weight on. And his son had never lifted more than him.

The boy was watching him. His father saw how the stark light made slashes and pits of his face. He looked away towards the mound of cold iron plates on the ends of the bar and slid on to the bench.

'On three give me a lift-off.'

'Okay.'

The father paused, his hands wrapped around the cold metal as he tried to put his mind into the right place. Any thoughts of weakness or failure or what might happen would mean he would not be able to do it. Thoughts like that would trap him under the bar. The weight would come crushing down on his chest and he would be humiliated, pinned until his son was able to come around and flick the whole thing sideways off him on to the concrete.

His son was looking down at him.

His father sucked in air. 'Okay. One, two, three!'

Even with his elbows locked straight the bar felt tremendously heavy. More than his own body-weight hanging above him. He watched it tremble as though a breeze had entered the garage. And then, slowly, he lowered it. He felt the crushing weight trying to rush down on to him, through him, but he held it. For a moment the bar touched his chest and bent his ribs inwards, and then he was trying to push it up and away.

It was too heavy. He got it so far, a hand's width, and then it stopped. He trembled and strained, his face red. His teeth ground together and his lips pulled back. His eyes screwed down into puckered holes.

'Push. Push!'

He heard his son's voice, but he was inside himself wrestling in his head with the weight. He felt it paused like a video picture, almost frozen, flickering between falling back and going forward. He felt his arms begin to shake, his muscles shiver and spasm. He knew that he was holding his breath and that was wrong but he had to. He had to have everything behind the weight, even the air. It all counted. He had to push it away.

Push.

Push.

Push.

Away.

Back up to where his son was waiting.

He felt something deep inside himself rip and tear. He was not precisely sure where it was, just somewhere deep in him, in his gut. A stabbing that twisted inside him. He heard himself cry out, all the trapped air flying out of him up into the shadows above. The weight fell back.

And then his son was helping him. Pulling the weight up and away from him. And then it was gone.

'You okay, Dad? Dad?'

He lay with his eyes closed. There were small silver lights blinking on and off in the darkness. He opened his eyes and his son's face hung above him where the weight had just been. He closed his eyes again.

'What is it? Are you okay?'

He lay for a time as if he was getting his breath back, and then he sat up. The pain moved inside him, sliding sideways like a living thing.

'Yeah. Think I just pulled a muscle. I should have warmed up more. Reckon I'll call it quits for tonight, eh?' He did not look up into his son's eyes.

'You sure you're okay?'

'Fine. I'll be good as gold in a few minutes.'

The father stood up and left the garage. He walked slowly. He was not breathing hard but sweat stood out on the darker skin beneath his eyes and on the slope of his nose. He did not want to go inside yet. Instead he walked over and stood next to the old pear tree. Behind him he could hear his son unloading the plates and pulling the bench press back into the corner. The metal legs scraped over the pale concrete. After a few minutes his son turned out the garage light and pulled down the door. Neither of them spoke, and the father did not look around.

After his son had walked back to the house and the door had closed, he stood alone in the darkness with only the light from the naked bulb. Deep inside him he could still feel the pain, small and sharp like a sliver of cold metal. Above him the stars were hard to see through the naked branches of the pear tree and he thought about how he would have to get around to taking it out. It was old and gave no pears that were worth eating. The night was bitter and in the morning he knew there would be frost on the grass.

family life

afterwards we went out to the kitchen and Maureen made me some eggs for breakfast. We'd only been together a couple of weeks. Short enough anyway that I still enjoyed watching her move around the place. She was wearing an old silk dressing gown with a picture of a crane on the back. It was frayed around the edges but still looked good on her. I remember, she had bare feet. Maureen moved from the fridge to the counter with a carton of eggs. She broke half a dozen into a glass bowl and whipped them up with a fork, and then she saw that I was watching her.

'What are you looking at?'

'You. Just thinking how good you look.'

She huffed air out through her nose and kept on whipping the egg. 'Hope you like your eggs well cooked.'

'Sure. That's fine.'

She served them up on toast and then sat down

opposite me at the table.

I was still looking at her. 'So what have you got planned today?'

She blinked slowly. 'You don't have to hang around, you know.'

'Sure. No. But I thought you might want to drive out somewhere. Go for a drive out of town.'

She looked sceptically towards the window where the day showed through overcast. It must have been nearly eleven already. Watching her, I reckoned that maybe she was thirty-seven or thirty-eight but it was hard to tell exactly and of course I hadn't asked. Those thin lines that smokers get were just starting to spread up from the edge of her top lip like collapsed under-runners. From the look on her face I could tell she was still undecided about going for a ride.

'I've got nothing I've gotta do today,' I said to encourage her. 'How about we drive out to the beach. We could have a picnic.'

She looked towards the window again and shrugged. 'Why not. But don't expect me to make any food. This lot's all you get, okay.'

After we'd finished eating, Maureen changed into a pair of black jeans and a pink fluffed-up top that I didn't think suited her. I didn't say anything, although I would have if we'd been together longer — but that top, it made her look like she was trying too hard to look younger than she was. We took my car which I'd cleaned and vacuumed the day before. The leather had that good new smell, and as we drove through town I was suddenly feeling better than I had in a long time. The radio was playing songs I remembered from when I first left school and started working, back before my divorce, when things had looked more promising. I reached over and put my hand on Maureen's knee.

'I've just gotta do something, okay,' she said. 'It'll only take five minutes, promise. Just turn left up here.'

She gave me directions through the eastern suburbs until I pulled the car up outside an old bay villa in a street close to the industrial part of town. No one had bothered painting the house in years or even mowing the lawns, and the guttering sagged down in places. It was what real estate agents would call a 'handyman's dream'. Maureen got out without a word and started up the path. I was curious and shadowed her around to the back door, expecting her to tell me to go back to the car. She didn't say anything, though. When she went in without knocking I followed.

Inside, the house was dim and the air carried the musty thickness of dogs past and present. I walked behind her through to the kitchen. A small dark-haired girl sat in the corner watching *The Wizard of Oz* on video. Even from where I was standing on the other side of the room I could hear the kid breathing. A slow rasp like someone filing the edge of a piece of sheet-metal. She looked up as we came in and then looked back at the screen.

I stood by the door and watched as Maureen went over and picked up the girl. 'Hello, there, Pumpkin. You been a good girl?' The little girl nodded and coughed deeply as if Maureen's picking her up had loosened something in her chest. 'What you been doing then?'

'We killed a mouse. Phil picked it up and threw it over the fence.'

Maureen frowned. 'Well, honey, maybe that mouse was

only sleeping.'

The little girl gave her a look like that was the stupidest thing she'd ever heard. 'It was dead. Phil hit it flat with his shoe.'

Maureen sighed and nodded and put the girl down. She went over and pulled the yellowed curtains away from the windows above the kitchen sink. There was leftover food on plates on the table and there was a bar-heater by the girl but where I was standing it was as cold as it was outside, maybe even colder. Maureen flicked on the jug and got down a packet of instant coffee from a cupboard without having to search.

She looked at me. 'You want a cup?'

'Sure.' I was keen to keep driving out to the beach but reckoned there was no point in pushing.

We were sitting drinking coffee and watching the video with the girl when a door closed somewhere in the house and a guy came to the door of the room and stood there looking in. He was short but not fat, with the wiry look that little guys have who keep the weight off by smoking or exercising a lot. The most distinctive thing about him was his hair. At some point he'd had hair plugs planted across the top of his brow to disguise his receding hair. Now that he was bald as a monk, the plugs were marooned there in the front like a row of pine trees on a barren ridge.

'My my, isn't this a pleasant family picture.'

Maureen frowned at him. 'Don't start anything stupid, Phil. I'm just here to check on Angela.'

'Sure you're not here to check up on me?'

'Just leave it alone, Phil.'

He came into the room, walking the way little guys do who want to seem bigger than they really are. He still hadn't so much as looked at me, and Maureen didn't introduce me or bother explaining what I was doing there in the kitchen drinking his coffee. It made me feel awkward. Phil sat down opposite, looking at Maureen who stood up and started making him a coffee without him asking. He watched her with a sort of half-smile.

At last he floated his eyes across to me. 'That your Nissan parked out the front?'

'Yeah.' And then because I didn't want to offend him I said, 'I've only had it a few months.'

'Right. I've been thinking of getting one of those myself.'

Behind me Maureen breathed out suddenly. 'Is that right, Phil? Are you gunna buy yourself a new car, are you?'

I twisted in my seat to look at her and was sorry that I had. Her face had hardened up so that she looked mean and older than I thought she was.

She looked back at me. 'Phil's lucky if he can afford new shoes.'

I wished she hadn't brought me into it, but Phil acted as if she hadn't said anything. 'How's she run?'

'Fine. No problems at all so far.'

Phil nodded like I'd told him everything there was to know about cars. 'And a reasonable price I bet.'

'Sure. Not too bad considering.'

There was no mistaking that he was the girl's father. They had the same brown eyes. Large eyes that curved down sleepily at the corners. Those eyes suited the girl, but somehow looked out of place on a wiry little guy like Phil with tattoos showing below the sleeves of his T-shirt.

'So whatdya do for a crust?' he asked.

'I'm an electrician.'

'Much work on, is there?'

'A fair bit. There's a lot of new houses going up.'

'Christsake, Phil,' said Maureen, sounding tired more than angry. 'Whatdya need to know for? We're just here to check on Angela and then we're going.'

'I'm just being social.' But he didn't ask me any more questions. He sat running his fingers over the wooden tabletop, caressing it like he was feeling for a flaw in the surface. I tried not to stare at the row of plugs across the front of his head.

Maureen brought Phil his coffee and then went and sat on the floor behind the girl, her legs out in front on either side, and started stroking the kid's hair. We all sat in silence and listened to the song about the yellow brick road.

When we'd finished our coffee, Phil asked where we were headed and I told him out to the beach. 'How about taking Angela and me along? We've been cooped up here and I reckon a walk along the beach would do her good.'

I looked over at Maureen for help. She just shrugged and looked away like she didn't care one way or the other. Of course I didn't want to take them along. My plan had been to go with Maureen to the beach, maybe have a picnic and lie down together on a private spot in the dunes. If it had just been Phil asking to tag along I could have turned him down flat, but of course the girl was all rolled up with him.

'We were just going to take a walk.'

'A walk's just what we need isn't it, Ange?'

The girl kept staring at the screen, aware that no reply was necessary.

I looked from Phil to the kid and then back at

Maureen. The truth is I've never been good at saying no to people's faces. 'Sure. Why not?'

Which was how I found myself driving out to the beach with Maureen next to me in the passenger seat and Phil and the girl sitting in the back. The girl stared out the window and asked what things were and Maureen told her. Obvious things mostly, like advertising billboards and later clumps of toi toi and cattle-stops. I got the feeling that she already knew the answers but liked Maureen to explain. Phil didn't say a single word beyond complimenting me on how tidy I kept the inside of the car until we passed the sawmill on the edge of town out by the oxidation ponds.

'That's where I used to work. Harbidges' Lumber. For ten years I worked there.'

Maureen went all tight lipped again and turned her head to stare out the window. I looked at Phil in the rear-view mirror. 'Is that right?'

'It was good work until they got a new foreman a few years ago. That fat bastard had it in for me.'

'Sure. I know the type.'

'Kept harping on about every little thing that I did. Nothing was good enough for him.'

'Some blokes are like that.'

In the mirror I saw Phil's eyes flick towards the back of my head as though he was checking to see if I was taking the mickey. 'In the end he arranged it for me to get the sack. After ten years I didn't even get any redundancy.'

I nodded and muttered something I hoped sounded sympathetic. I also hoped that Phil had finished talking. I wasn't in the mood for his talk. I guess that even then I was thinking it might be possible to salvage something from the trip. Maureen and I might still get to spend some time alone. The girl coughed again, lots of little coughs that ran together into a deep hack. It was a strange sound coming from such a small kid, an old man's cough. A pack-a-day-for-forty-years cough. I wondered if anyone had thought to take her to the doctor's but didn't think it was my place to say anything.

Maureen looked across at me. 'I haven't been to the beach for ages. I used to all the time when I was younger, but I haven't been for ages and ages.' She smiled and reached over and put her hand on top of mine where it was holding the gear stick. In the rear-view mirror I could see Phil watching us.

Mine was the only car in the expanse of tarseal that overlooked the beach. In January you couldn't get a park here, but now we were the only ones. The sun was starting to show through the clouds every now and then, and I thought that it might not be too bad even with Phil and the girl. I had forgotten about the wind though. As soon as we got out of the car the onshore easterly breeze cut into our skin.

'It's all right,' said Maureen. 'We've got more clothes.' She fished some jackets out of the bag she'd packed back at Phil's house and helped the girl dress. I got an old coat I used in winter on building sites out of the boot. Only Phil didn't dress for the wind. He was still wearing the black jeans and the T-shirt he'd been wearing at the house, and I wondered how he could stand the cold. He waited next to my car while we dressed, and then we all walked down the track to the sand, the girl and me and Maureen in the front and Phil trailing behind.

I was surprised but the girl perked up straight away. She found a stick and began drawing big pictures in the sand. The tide was out and the wind was flattening the tops off the breakers. Phil walked ahead up the beach towards the rocks, and Maureen and I followed slowly. When he was far enough ahead I took her hand and pulled her close. I kissed her on the lips. Maureen's mouth was warm and I slipped my hand inside her jacket so that it cupped one breast. She didn't move my hand away or step back. After a while, Maureen put her arm around my waist underneath my jacket and tucked herself in close.

As we walked, the girl ran down to the edge of the water, occasionally shouting back at us to look at things she'd found washed up.

'I'm sorry about Phil.'

'It's okay. I don't mind. I could've said no.'

'He beat up that foreman. Waited for him one day outside his house and then beat him senseless with a soft-ball bat. Phil was lucky he didn't kill him.'

'What happened?'

'Phil lied at the trial said that the guy had threatened to hurt me and Angela. But he still got two years. He's only been out a few months.'

I looked towards where Phil was climbing nimbly over the rocks which marked the end of the beach. It wasn't much of a stretch to imagine him waiting in the shadows down the side of someone's house, an angry little man with a baseball bat and a chip on his shoulder. As I watched, Phil turned and started waving urgently back at us. He'd obviously found something and seemed excited. He called out but his words were blown inland by the wind.

Maureen sighed and moved apart from me, and we walked across the sand to the rocks, and then over them towards where Phil was standing. She walked carefully as though every rock wasn't to be trusted and might move beneath her feet. I followed her, and the girl followed us all.

Phil had found a seal tangled in part of a fishing net. There was a terrible smell and at first I thought it was dead. It lay there black and still and stinking, covered in flies, but as I moved closer it opened one eye and looked at me.

'It's tangled up,' said Phil unnecessarily. And then to me, 'Give me a hand and we can get the net off.'

The truth was if I'd been alone I probably would have kept right on walking. The seal stank, and there were flies and other crawling insects. I could see at least two deep cuts on its flank, probably from the rocks, and I could tell that the net was wrapped good and tight around its flippers and head. Any fool could see it was pretty close to being dead. But Phil was already down beside it, pulling at the net, and so I joined him.

I used the work knife I always kept on my belt for electrical work to cut away at the nylon. Although the seal lay still, I was wary and stayed well down from the business end. Behind me, Maureen was explaining to the girl what we were doing, that we were trying to help the seal. The girl stood still and stared at us with her large brown eyes.

When the net finally slipped free the seal just lay there. At least one of the cuts on its body was really deep and looked infected, and I wondered how long the seal had lain there on the rocks in the sun.

'Why doesn't it swim away?'

'It will, honey.'

Maureen looked across at Phil but he just looked

worried. He began trying to coax the seal back into the
water. He started pushing it with his hands and then with
his shoe, but the seal simply lay there with its eyes closed,
breathing slowly. The seal's lack of willingness to help itself
seemed to anger Phil. He was suddenly yelling and pushing
at it roughly with his foot.

'Move! Come on, move, you bastard. Move.'

But the seal just lay there and in the end Phil swore
loudly and moved away over the rocks towards the car
park.

'Is the seal going to die?'

Maureen sighed. 'It might, love. We'll just have to wait
and see.' The girl took Maureen's hand and they turned
away and set off slowly after Phil.

I went down to the water where thick brown kelp
sloshed on the surface and tried to wash the stench of seal
off my hands, but it didn't work. I needed soap and my
hands became numb in the surging water.

The smell of seal still hung around me when I caught
up to Maureen and the girl who were walking along the
beach towards the car.

'I'm cold,' said the girl, and she burrowed into her
mother.

The clouds had finally decided to settle in and the wind
had picked up. Sand was starting to move across the beach
at ankle height in a rustling sheet.

As we walked I could see Phil ahead. He must have
been walking quickly because he was already up in the car
park, standing by my car. He'd picked up something, a
large piece of driftwood, from the beach, and as I watched
he raised it over his head and brought it down heavily on
the bonnet. The wind plucked away the sound and blew it

away from us so that the impact was silent.

It took me a moment to realise what was happening, and then I swore and started to run across the sand as Phil began to rain heavy blows down on my car. I couldn't take my eyes off him and stumbled several times in the deep dry sand of the dunes. I was running up the track from the beach when I heard the windscreen crash and splinter, and then a panel popped in as like a softball player he brought the wood in a sideways swing into the passenger door.

He must have heard me coming but stayed focused on the car.

I finally got to him and grabbed the driftwood from behind as he raised it up over his head for another blow. I pulled and the wood came out of his hands surprisingly easily. He turned to face me and I considered hitting him with the wood but didn't have something like that in me and simply threw it as far as I could. For a moment we stood staring at each other, and then Phil closed in on me and grabbed me around the chest like a wrestler.

'Fight me,' he hissed in my ear. 'Fight me, you bastard.'

I knew, even then, that he wasn't really angry at me, just at everything that had gone wrong in his life. Still I wasn't going to let him hurt me, and clasped one arm around his neck and twisted my body so that I had him in a headlock. I could feel his wiry arms still wrapped around me. We did a kind of jerky little tango over the parking spaces until I lost my footing and we both fell to the ground. It was only good luck that meant Phil fell backwards and I fell on top. But by that time Phil had gone limp. There was no fight left in him any more.

'Let him go! Let him go. You're hurting him!'

Maureen had run up from the beach and was yelling at

me. She hit me across the shoulder with her fist, a blow that hurt more than anything Phil had done to me and that left a bruise I didn't discover until the next day. The truth was though, I was glad she was there. I had no idea what to do next. I relaxed my grip on Phil and stood up.

Phil just lay there on his back, staring up at the clouded sky and breathing hard.

I stepped back and watched as Maureen helped him to his feet. He was unsteady, and when he was standing she wrapped her arms around him. I saw that his head only came up to just below her chin.

'Don't worry. Everything is going to turn out fine.' She was crying and holding him.

The little girl had come up from the beach with Maureen. She stood staring and then moved in closer, spreading her arms wide to hug both her parents around their waists. Phil's hand dropped to the top of her head. She turned her face and gave me an accusing look as if everything was my fault.

There was nothing I could do. What could I do? I looked back towards the beach and then back at the three of them holding each other in the windswept car park. My hands were numb from the water, and I was starting to shiver from the cold and I guess from the shock. I smelt of seal. I didn't know what to do, so I went and sat in my beat-up car with window glass like rough diamonds scattered over the seats. I sat there and waited for Maureen and her family to finish and join me for the drive back to the city.

I didn't lay any charges against Phil with the police, or anything like that. The way I thought about it afterwards was that things had just caught up with him. I'd never felt like that myself but I'd been close and could understand it. Insurance paid up on the car after I reported it had been vandalised.

I didn't see Maureen again before I went to work up in Auckland for Radcliffe's, an electrical wholesaling outfit. The building sector had gone into recession and the work wiring new houses had dried up down south. At Radcliffe's I was what they called a 'key account manager' which was the flash way of saying a salesman. They gave me a car and cellphone and forty grand a year plus commissions. The money came in steadier than when I was working for myself, and it wasn't an office job. I got to meet a lot of good people. I guess you could say I was happy with the way things had panned out. Happy enough anyway.

I had girlfriends, a couple of them pretty long term. I even lived with a woman called Penny for a while, but somehow that hadn't worked out. But I wasn't unhappy living alone in an apartment close enough to work that I didn't have to stress about the traffic.

I saw Phil again about a month ago. I was in a supermarket, standing in front of rows of different soups, trying to decide what I wanted for dinner, when I looked across and there he was right next to me. He was wearing jeans and a long-sleeved shirt that hid his tattoos. If anything he'd lost more hair, but the row of plugs was still there across the front of his head. I thought I could smell alcohol on his breath. It was ten o'clock on a Saturday morning.

'Gidday, look who it is,' he said, and came the few steps towards me with his hand outstretched.

'Hi, Phil.'

I'm not sure if he remembered my name or if Maureen

had even told it to him. He was with a redheaded woman who must have been fifteen years younger than him. She stood apart and eyed me in a bored way.

Because we had absolutely nothing else to talk about I asked if he'd seen Maureen lately.

'She's still down south. Hooked up with some builder. Not a bad bloke though.'

'And how's Angela?'

He smiled and I was struck by his brown eyes. They were eyes too pretty for a guy like Phil. 'Angela's good. She's right into horses — jumping. Bloody good at it too. I try and visit her a couple of times a year. I call her.'

'I'm glad to hear that.'

'She starts high school next year. Can you believe it.' He shook his head in a slow, disbelieving kind of way.

'She seemed like a nice kid.'

'Yeah. She's great.'

He looked across at the redhead and then back at me and raised his eyebrows. 'Well, gotta go, eh. Don't wanta keep the women waiting. You know how they get.' He grinned. We shook hands again and they walked away down the aisle towards the tills.

I finished doing my shopping and wheeled my groceries out in to the car park where a few drops of rain were starting to fall. Phil was sitting in the front of an old Commodore with the redhead. They were parked in the handicapped spot near the door. He got out when he saw me, and came over.

'I just wanted to say that I'm sorry about the car.'

'Sure. Forget about it. Ancient history.'

'If you were out of pocket, I've got some money now.'

'No. That's fine. Insurance.'

'You got kids?' he asked.

'No.'

He nodded but seemed reluctant to turn around. 'You know, just between you and me, I worry that I'm not much of an excuse for a father.'

'I suppose you try your best.'

'Yeah. I try. I guess that's what counts.' But he didn't seem convinced.

The rain was starting to fall harder. Phil turned suddenly and without saying anything else walked away, leaving me standing alone in the car park. I got into my car, started the engine and began the short drive home to my empty apartment.

The Raft

Shiny shiny bursts of silver sparkling behind the green leaves pretty as anything he has seen before behind him there is the sound of hammering and he knows he shouldn't they'll be mad and may growl but pushing through the bushes crawling when he has to so that his hands are dirty until he can see it properly and he has never seen anything so beautiful and he claps his hands in delight the gate pushes open at his touch and the concrete is hot on his bare feet and it is so bright that he squints his eyes and holds up his hand with the sticking-plaster thumb to shade his eyes as he reaches out to feel the beauty feels himself toppling forward

sudden silence

looking up he can see himself reflected in the sky

Rain falls the entire time they are driving to the bach. Tonia will say this for The Coast: they know how to do rain. Nothing pissy or drizzly, just pregnant drops that fall like they mean business, as if they have a firm destination in mind. The windscreen wipers move too quickly and are making her feel ill. Her right ear is sore and she readjusts the sweatshirt she is using for a pillow. Andrew does not look at her. He has not spoken the whole trip. He drives with his mind outside the car, staring past the windscreen at the late afternoon rain and the black eel that is the highway. If that's the way he wants it, she thinks. She closes her eyes again. She curls her small body down further in the front seat and tries to hear each raindrop as it hits the roof of the car.

She wakes in an almost darkness to find that she is alone. Confused, she sits up. How long has the engine been switched off? It could have been hours. No, not hours, the inside of the car is still warm, probably just a few minutes then. Where the hell is Andrew? It is raining harder than ever, the noise in the car is deafening, as though the cats and dogs her mother never failed to mention on days like this are making fatal landings just above her head. She sees now that the car is parked almost at the front door of the bach, at the end of the two ruts that pass for a drive through the knee-high lawn. But there are no lights on inside, no sign of Andrew. She stares out at the weatherboard house chocked up on its high piles like spindly legs. It is, she thinks, ugly. Typically, Andrew's father bought it cheap with no thought of aesthetics. It used to be an old forestry hut which became surplus to requirements. She twists herself in the seat to look behind but cannot see Andrew. Nor the lake. The rain falls like a stage curtain.

She is startled when Andrew reappears beside the car.

He is holding the hood of his jacket forward from his face as he taps on the window. He gestures impatiently for her to follow. She opens the door and her jeans are immediately soaked. He runs ahead of her across the grass and up the steps to the narrow porch.

'Where were you?'

'Getting the key.' He holds up a small glass jar covered in dirt, inside which is a single key. A slater drops to the ground and disappears over the edge of the porch.

The door opens to darkness and a faint whiff of something ripe and foul. Tonia waits while Andrew feels his way along the wall and out of sight. She can hear him cursing and a hollow thump as something falls.

'Are you okay?'

Her answer is the lights coming on. The white light of naked bulbs spills out on to the porch and shows her a clutter of old shoes. Hats of all sorts dangle from hooks, and there is a stiff oilskin hanging like something shed. Remnants of Andrew's family — his father, his mother, and his older sister Alice who now lives in Sydney.

Andrew is swearing. 'What's the matter?'

'The roof is leaking. Come and look.'

An ugly brown stain has spread across the ceiling of the lounge, making the plaster swell and sag. There is another stain over by the wall close to the two doors which she vaguely remembers lead to the bunk room and his parents' room, although she is not sure which is which now. Tonia has been here only twice before. Once when she came back from England that first time, and they spent three or four days here over Christmas. It was hot and they slept with the windows open and mosquito coils burning in the dark. There were screens over the windows to keep the sandflies out but even so they still found their way in and bit at her ankles and wrists. Each night she and Andrew had started off in separate bunks but ended up together, afraid to make even the slightest sound in case his parents, asleep in the next room, should hear.

She remembers little of the second trip, apart from the fact that she was pregnant and could eat anything as long as it was plain dry crackers. She'd spent a lot of time throwing up into the toilet and, just for variety, on to the garden. And then Liam was born, and because he was a fractious baby and, even when he was older, whined like crazy during car trips longer than down to the super-market, they had not come here again.

Andrew is still investigating the damage. 'This couch is absolutely soaked. I think the carpet might have to be replaced. Fuck knows about the floor. The boards are most likely rotted through by now.'

She does not feel that he needs her to comment. 'I'll go out and get the bags,' she says.

'There's nothing much we can do about this tonight anyway.'

'Maybe there are some extra towels?'

He shakes his head. 'We'll need buckets.'

In the end it takes two buckets, three ice-cream containers and an old green glass vase which they find under the sink to catch all the drips. They arrange them on the couch, the kitchen breakfast-bar, the green Formica table and strategically around the sodden floor. After they are finished she finds another leak in the bunk room — the door on the left, she has discovered — and puts a glass bowl underneath the slow drip of water. She wrinkles her nose at the smell of rotting carpet.

'I need a drink,' says Andrew. 'Do you want one?'

'No.' She stands and watches while he makes himself a gin and tonic. He is casually careful about how much gin he pours.

'What?' he demands.

'Nothing.'

'If you're going to start . . .'

'I'm tired. I think I'll go to bed.' She takes her bags and goes into the bunk room. She lies in the darkness, listening to the endless rain and to the metered *plop plop plop plop* of the drips falling into the bowl.

After a long time she hears Andrew go into the other bedroom and close the door.

He is swimming slowly across the surface of a vast black lake. He opens his eyes and looks down through water the colour of weak tea. The light travels down below him but then is quickly twisted and swallowed. There is the familiar feeling of hanging near the ceiling of a huge room with walls he can't see. A hollow place. Below him long shapes trail up, strands of weed from the bottom.

Something moves. A thing that does not match the rhythm of the weed's slow sway. Something sleek and black. And then it is gone. He falters in his stroke and floats face down, turning his head from side to side to try and see clearly. But whatever it was it is hidden now. There is only green-black water and weed trailing up from the bottom.

Raising his head, he starts to tread water. He looks around. Dark clouds have gathered, the makings of a thunderstorm, and the shore is still a long way off, barely visible. The clouds are piling up in the sky and the light is fading. He is tired and unsure of how long he has been in the water. He is stone cold and the shore never seems to get any nearer. Something is down there amongst the weed. Something much bigger than him that is watching as he thrashes across the surface, biding its time.

He looks down again past his pale dangling legs. The weed is much closer now, as though it has grown up in a sudden spurt to touch him. Brushing his feet. He pulls his legs away and suddenly knows without doubt that whatever it is waiting down there is rushing up towards him. Here it comes. Fast. Mouth agape. Up through the weed and the dark water. He just can't see it yet. He starts thrashing wildly but has suddenly forgotten how to swim. He is like a bug trapped on the surface of the lake.

It is rushing up fast through the dark water. Any moment and he will feel the creature's teeth sink into his flesh. He screams.

It is the terror that always wakes him.

Andrew lies on his back and listens to the sound of his own tattered breathing. He is tangled in the sheets and dripping wet so that he thinks for a moment the ceiling above his bed has sprung another leak. It is hot sweat. He wonders if he has been screaming in his sleep again, but Tonia does not stir in the other room. It is still raining, and he has no idea what the time is. There is no clock and he has stopped wearing a watch. Even when he climbs out of bed and turns on the light the feeling of being hunted stays with him. His sweat dries cold. He wraps a musty woollen blanket from the closet around his shoulders and goes into the kitchen.

He rolls a cigarette without looking at his hands, and stands staring out at the rain from the bay window that was added on to the house after it was moved. On the window sill a thin white fuzz of mould is growing like fine new hair. The air inside is heavy, damp. The tattered couch and the armchair with the tiger-patterned throw-rug give up their moisture. The carpet seeps. Everything smells of the damp which comes from the furniture but also from the lake and from the dripping bush behind the property where moisture creeps like a squatter, waiting only for them to go before it slips back inside. Careful not to wake Tonia he rummages in a kitchen drawer until he finds a lighter.

Of course he knows where the dream comes from. His father built the raft when Andrew was seven, and promised ten dollars the first time Andrew swam out to it. At seven, those forty metres had looked like the Tasman. That summer he practised every day up and down the shore, but as soon as his feet left the bottom he'd panic and turn back. He could swim well enough; that wasn't his problem. His problem was Terry-Fucking-Mulligan. Terry's parents used to own the bach three down, the one with the green front door. Terry was twelve and a natural-born asshole. He told Andrew that there was a giant monster that lived in the lake. Always the inventive one, he called it The Creature. Said it was half giant eel, half sea dinosaur left over from when the lake was joined to the ocean. Andrew still remembers the look on Terry's face when he told him how he'd seen The Creature attacking his uncle. That kid's eyes bulged. Actually his uncle did get cramp one year and almost drowned, but Terry was just winding him up. Little prick.

On the last day before they were due to go home Andrew had caged his fear and made it halfway to the raft before something brushed his leg under the water — weed or a stick. He froze up, screamed so much that he almost drowned. His father swam out and pulled him back to shore, still hysterical. It was one of the most embarrassing things that had ever happened to him. He can still remember parents and kids from the other baches standing around looking down at him as he lay gasping and sobbing on the shore. He didn't swim at all for a couple of years and didn't swim out to the raft until he was fourteen. By that time he was too proud to claim his father's ten dollars and they both pretended they'd forgotten all about it.

As he smokes, the rain runs in sheets down the outside of the window. He still does not know what the time is. Maybe midnight, one o'clock. He does not think he has been asleep for that long. As his eyes adjust to the darkness he can make out the sagging belly of the wire fence and the pale gouge of the shingle road and the blacker emptiness of the lake beyond. There are five other baches clustered together here in this inlet near the end of the road but the others are, of course, empty. August is exactly the wrong time of year to come to the lake. Why he let Tonia talk him into coming he doesn't know. She said it would help and he'd almost believed her. There is another flurry of rain and the edges of everything shift and swim. There are, he thinks, no straight lines left in the world any more.

He is startled when car headlights shine through the window, lighting up the room. For a moment he has a Peter Pan shadow. He steps back from the window as a car pulls up behind his and people get out. He cannot tell who they are. Two dark figures hurry across the lawn and the unlocked door bangs open. There are voices in the hallway. And then the lights come on and he is face to face with his father. They both stand frozen.

'What are you doing here?'

His father grimaces. 'I could ask you the same thing.'

And then his mother is between them, flustered, and trying to smooth things over. 'It's all right, Bill. Calm down. I was going to say something but I didn't want to upset you . . . the truth is that . . .' She stops, confused.

'What's going on? Mum?'

'Don't get angry. Both of you. I can explain . . . oh dear.'

'This wasn't my idea, Andrew.' His father hasn't moved from the doorway.

'Just turn around and go then.'

'Christ, I do own the place!' Bill barks.

'Stop it, you two. I'm sorry. We shouldn't have come.'

And suddenly Tonia is in the room, pulling a dressing gown over her pyjamas. 'It was my idea,' she says lightly. 'I asked them to come.' She kisses Shirley on the cheek and hugs his father who stands stiff as an old tree. 'It's good to see you, Bill. You're looking well.'

Bill grimaces again. 'I look bloody awful.'

Tonia smiles. 'Either way it's been too long.' She turns back to Andrew. 'Shirley and I decided that we all needed to spend some time together.'

'It might not have been a good idea,' says his mother, looking around like a lost child.

'It was a stupid idea,' he says too loudly and he sees her stiffen.

'Don't talk to your mother like that,' Bill snaps.

'Your father didn't know you were going to be here, dear.'

'Well, we're not. We're leaving.'

His mother is suddenly wide eyed. 'It's the middle of the night.'

'I don't need my wife and my mother sneaking around behind my back. Christ, Tonia, what were you thinking? Help me pack the bags.'

'Pack your own bloody bag. I'm staying.'

He glares at her. 'Suit yourself.'

He goes into the bedroom and returns with his suitcase. He has not bothered to zip it shut, and clothes dangle from its mouth. The last thing he sees as he leaves is Tonia, Shirley and Bill standing silently, like those buskers he can't stand who only move when you put money in their hat. He slams the door behind him.

The car wheels spin briefly on the wet grass and then he is reversing quickly around his parents' car on to the road and driving away.

Tonia is still in bed when she hears Andrew return just after dawn. Shirley and Bill are still asleep. She pulls on shorts and a blue and yellow thermal top, and goes out to where their car is parked by the lake. It has stopped raining, although there is no sign of the sun, and dark clouds hang low over the lake. Andrew has taken his shoes off and is standing knee deep in the water, staring out at a wooden raft moored out from the shore. As soon as she stops moving the sandflies start to swarm around her exposed skin.

'Going for a swim?'

Andrew does not turn around. 'I wanted to feel what the water was like.'

'Well?'

'Fucking cold.' There is a pause. 'I didn't change my mind, if that's what you're thinking. A tree's washed down and blocked the ford. Must have happened just after they crossed.'

There is another pause during which Tonia can hear the slap of the lake against the stones and the sandflies begin to bite her in earnest. She should have remembered and worn long pants. She slaps at the back of her hand and sees a bloated sandfly smear across her skin. 'Where'd you sleep?'

'The back seat. My neck's killing me.'

'Serve you right for insisting we buy a Fiat.'

'They *are* economical.'

She can't help smiling and he turns and looks at her for the first time. She sees his raw morning-after eyes. 'Least it's not raining now,' she says.

He glances up at the low ash-coloured sky. 'It was a stupid thing you and Mum did.'

'I don't think . . .' she begins.

Andrew raises his voice. 'No, let me finish. I can make my own decisions about who I do and don't see.'

'Christ, he's your father.'

'I'm thirty-eight years old. I don't need a father any more. Especially not him.'

'Listen to yourself. You've got to move on from what happened.'

'Move on to where? Where am I supposed to be going, Tonia? Tell me? Where is this mythical destination?'

Andrew is yelling now and she feels her stomach bunch in what has become a reflex. Andrew stops and looks back towards the lake. She waits.

He speaks gently. 'Even when I'm with people, I'm not with them. You know what I mean?'

'No, but tell me. Please.'

'It's like I hear people laughing and saying things that I should be interested in but I'm not. It's all happening way, way over there.' He gestures over the black water. 'And I'm just not part of anything.'

'Then what are you going to do about it?'

Andrew shrugs. 'I don't know.'

Now is the time. She will say what she has been planning to say for weeks, what she brought him to the bach to say. 'I can't live with "I don't know" any more.'

He turns to look at her again. 'What does that mean?'

'Until you sort yourself out I need to be by myself.'

'By yourself meaning not with me?'

She nods.

'For how long?

'As long as it takes.'

'So our marriage is over — just like that.'

She thinks how small and alone he looks standing in the water. His feet must be numb.

'Not necessarily. It depends.'

'On what?

'On *you*. Everything depends on you. Andrew, this is best for both of us.'

He kicks angrily at the water and ripples flee from his foot. 'Don't pretend you're thinking about me.'

'You're right. I'm not any more. That's the point.'

And suddenly a bird, a shag perhaps, long and black, is flying low across the water. They both turn their heads to watch its silent progress. It vanishes over the trees and she sighs. 'Our son died. Liam died.'

'I know that,' he says, breathing out on all the words so that his voice is like a sudden breeze between them.

'Do you? Do you really?'

'I carried his coffin. I held his cold hand all that first endless night.'

'Look me in the eye, Andrew, and tell me that you're not expecting him to come out from that bach any minute in his pyjamas and come running over here.'

Andrew starts to cry. His shoulders hunch but she is unrelenting.

'Isn't that what you're expecting? Isn't it?'

'Of course! That's natural. He's only just died.'

'It's been over a year since Liam died. Fourteen long months. I've said my goodbyes. You should too.'

'You're trying to forget him!' he accuses.

She shakes her head. 'I grieve for him every day but we've got to get on with living our lives.'

'I can still feel his tiny hand in mine. It's so cold.'

'Liam is *dead*. He was four years old and he died. We were unlucky.'

'It wasn't luck!' Andrew looks accusingly back at the bach.

'Either way, he's dead. You have to learn what that means.'

Without waiting for a reply, she turns and walks away. When she gets to the porch she looks back. Andrew is still standing in the water, staring out at the raft. He seems to be waiting for something, but for what she cannot imagine.

Andrew is driven inside by the latest downpour. He has heard his father chopping kindling out in the lean-to. His mother and Tonia murmur from the bedroom. He calls the nearest service station, who refer him to the local council. The guy who eventually answers the phone says he might be able to send someone with a winch to look at the ford but he isn't sure when they'll be able to get around to clearing it, certainly not today. He pronounces certainly with a drawn-out rolled southern 'rrr'. They're flat out with landslides up and down the highway. The man helpfully suggests that the ford might clear itself with the next heavy rain. He takes the number of the bach and promises to get back to them.

Andrew makes himself a cup of tea. The kettle's insides are thick with minerals.

'Forecast says it might clear up later today.'

His father has come in from the lean-to. The door is open behind him and the noise of the rain is loud. Andrew watches him out of the corner of his eye without fully turning. His father has a pile of kindling cradled in his arms which he drops noisily by the wood burner. Shards of wood cling to his bush-shirt. Andrew can smell the gum sap from the freshly split wood.

'If the rain lets up I might go for a walk later on.' His father's hair needs cutting where it clumps above his ears. Andrew is aware of him brushing at the bush-shirt with his large builder's hands, and water and shards of wood falling to the carpet. 'Maybe up to the big totara. Do you want to come? We could talk.' He is breathing too hard. He closes the door and takes a pill from a container in his shirt pocket.

'No. I'll stay here. The guy from the council might call back about the ford.'

Andrew hears his father begin to stack the wood around the burner, drying it out. He takes his tea and stares out the window and listens to the broken-drum sound of wood on wood. Because of the rain the surface of the lake is even darker than normal. Something to do with the minerals and plant matter washed down from the bush. There is no wind and the water is dead flat. Each raindrop falls heavily, hitting the cast-iron surface and then jumping high. At either end of the narrow stone beach the thick bush crowds down to the lake. Trees lean out on improbable angles, making dark half-tunnels; places where the rain does not fall on the water with the same steady rhythm but dances to its own random beat. Tangled bush-lawyer hang like ropes. Moss and mould and lichen cover the earth and cling to the trunks of the trees.

Behind him his father has stopped stacking the wood. Andrew does not turn around but stares rigidly out at the rain. The bach, the lake, the bush, everything feels saturated with decay; the undoing of the dead and of the only half-dead things. His father goes into his bedroom and closes the door without a word.

Andrew thinks back to a conversation he had with Tonia weeks ago now. Months? He has lost track of the connection between time and events. She was putting away groceries anyway, and he was sitting at the kitchen bench just watching. Of course the house was too still.

Half an hour earlier she had led him by the hand, like a child, from the supermarket and helped him gently into the passenger seat of their car. Things just seem to set him off for no real reason.

'You should call your father back,' she had said, opening the fridge and putting away the new butter.

'I can't.'

'This isn't going to help. You know that, Andrew.'

She was using her gentle but insistent voice. The one that she used when she proposed to him. He remembers her dark hair brushing the back of her neck as she moved around the kitchen. She was wearing a white T-shirt, jeans and summer sandals and looked beautiful. Summer then. At least five months ago.

Fresh tears had blurred the cupboard, blurred Tonia so that she was swimming towards him. She held him again. Back then she always seemed to be holding him, like scaffolding put up to stop a fire-gutted building collapsing entirely.

Even in her arms he couldn't help but listen. He still spends all his time in their house listening. He is always on the verge of hearing footsteps running over the polished floorboards in the hallway. Or high laughter. The tears of a scraped shin. But no one trips on the steps any more and doors hang on their hinges unslammed. Tonia has tried to talk about moving when the time is right.

In the kitchen she had stepped back, letting him go. 'It's as bad for him,' she said, 'maybe worse.'

'It's not worse!' He had hated the idea.

'Okay. Different. But still terrible though.'

'I don't know how I feel about him any more.'

'We agreed that you should spend some time together. Go away to the bach. Fish.'

'No.'

He pulled her in again. She was small but solid in his arms, and he had wet her shoulder with his tears. He remembers her beginning to kiss his neck and he had pulled away, turned and walked out of the kitchen.

They have not made love since Liam died. She has tried but he has turned aside. The implications are too many, too huge. She amazes him every day with her unbending strength. How does she stay so strong, so whole? How does she seem to be getting better when every day he feels as if he is slipping deeper into something dark that clings and sucks him under? For him there are only bad days and days that are worse.

'I don't know what to say to him.'

'What did you used to talk about?'

'I don't know. I can't remember.'

And it is true. He still can't remember what he used to talk about with his father. He stares hopelessly around the bach as though looking for a clue — the wood stacked neatly by the burner; faded prints on the walls; an ancient bar-heater — and then he sees the old rods by the door. He finds an image of himself and his father out on the lake. They were floating in the old aluminium dinghy. It was a sunny day and every now and then one of them reached down to bail water out of the bottom with a yellow detergent bottle cut in half. But in his memory they are not talking. The only sound he can conjure up is the scrape of the plastic bailer on the bottom of the boat and the splash of water being returned to the lake. His father and he are just sitting there.

Just sitting silently out on the lake waiting for the fish to bite.

Tonia and Shirley have gone for a walk around the edge of the lake towards the big totara. They have been talking all morning. About Bill's health, about Tonia's work, about Liam. Shirley stops walking, turns to her and asks, 'How is Andrew? Really. It's been so long since he's even called on the phone.'

'Where to start? He's angry, confused, belligerent, possibly alcoholic, masochistic, sadistic, depressive, emotionally and sometimes physically violent . . . I could go on all day.'

Shirley sighs and looks suddenly small and older than sixty-three. Her shoulders and face are too thin. 'He's grieving.'

'That's what I used to think too, but now I believe he's doing something else.'

'What?'

'He's like that ford.' She gestures up the road. 'All his emotions are dammed up in a great big pool but what we see is only what bursts out under all the pressure.'

'The ford will clear.'

'It's not a perfect analogy,' Tonia says.

'Counselling, maybe . . .'

'He did go to one session. Told the therapist he was "fine", "good as gold", and walked out. At first he was just quiet, still inside, thinking.'

Shirley gives a pale smile. 'Even as a boy he was a thinker.'

'He stopped going down to his office, didn't return calls from clients, started watching a lot of television. He never wanted to talk about Liam until one day I got a box and put all Liam's toys out in the garage. That was the first time he ever hit me.'

'Oh, my dear. I'm so sorry.'

'I was so stunned I didn't know what to do and then he hugged me and started howling. We were both standing there in the garage crying like babies. It's been over a year, and there's a stupid stuffed fish that my sister got Liam for his birthday sitting in the corner of the lounge. Liam never even liked it and Andrew still won't let me touch the thing.'

'I didn't raise him to hit.'

'He really thinks he should be this way. Like the war widow who wears black for the rest of her life, even though she was only married a month.'

Shirley pats her on the arm. 'They say time heals all wounds.'

'And a stitch in time saves nine. And have you heard that a rolling stone gathers no moss?'

Shirley blinks twice. 'Sorry, you've lost me. . .'

Irritated, Tonia starts walking again. There are ripples on the lake where small insects alight on the surface and loud plops as fish rise. Shirley follows her like a kicked puppy. When they get to the totara Tonia says, 'I want you to know I don't blame Bill. I did for a while but now I think that if it had been me or Andrew there that afternoon it wouldn't have changed anything. Liam was a boisterous, loud, beautiful four-year-old boy who was never in the same place for more than two seconds.'

Shirley cannot meet her eye. 'We were meant to be looking out for him.'

'Bill was meant to be.'

'I only popped down to the butcher's.'

'Once Liam learnt how to open doors, a week didn't go by when one of the neighbours didn't find him out on the street or playing in their garden. Liam was a storm in the shape of a little boy. He had me on tenterhooks the whole time.' Shirley starts to cry and Tonia holds her but keeps talking. 'I used to worry about him all the time, torture myself imagining all the ways he could get killed: run over by a car; sticking his head in a supermarket bag; strangling on the cord for the blinds . . . It sounds wrong, but for a small part of me it was almost a relief to know that the worst had happened and I didn't have to worry any more.'

She steps back and cups Shirley's crumpled face in her

hands and feels the soft sag of the old woman's skin and the tears that begin to pool in her palms. 'Listen to me, Shirley. Really listen. Liam came out of my body; no one loved him more than me, no one, not even Andrew, and *I* don't hold Bill, or you, responsible. You both loved him. I never doubted that. It was bad luck plain and simple.'

They stand and hold each other next to the trunk of the lone totara and cry, and above them the sun comes out for the first time in days. For a long time neither of them notices.

It is almost midday and the sun has come out hot. The clouds have broken up and blown east so that the sky is blue above the green of the bush. His mother and Tonia are off somewhere walking, and Bill is up on the roof hammering on new sheets of iron where the old stuff has rusted through. Andrew goes back inside where it seems dark after the stark sunlight and grabs a beach towel with all the softness washed out of it years ago. It is a short walk across the road and down the path to the shingle beach. He walks along the edge of the lake until he is standing opposite the raft.

Swimming to the raft was, is, a family tradition. He has never come here when everyone hasn't gone out to the raft at least once. Even his mother swam out in her baggy one-piece, moving through the water like an oil-sodden bird with her lazy side-stroke. Swimming to the raft was one of those tests of membership and fidelity that every family has whether they are aware of it or not. Then again he has never been here in August and he knows that the water is shockingly cold. But maybe that is what he needs now — a shock.

He takes off his shirt and kicks his shoes aside. The

water-smooth stones press into the soles of his feet. The
lake closes around his calves and makes him gasp. This
water flows down straight from the Alps and the lake is
deep. The sound of his father's hammering carries across
the road, and looking back he can see the old man
crouching, hammer raised, looking over towards where he
is standing. Andrew does not give any sign that he knows
he is being watched, but turns back to the lake and begins
to wade out and the shore quickly drops away.

The cold squeezes his thighs but it feels good to be able
to focus on another pain. He stands with the water at the
top of his legs and waits, breathing slowly in and out,
listening to the sound of his breath, anticipating the cold
clench of the water on his body. And then he throws
himself forward and feels the shards slashing along his
chest and sides and against the top of his scalp. It is colder
than he even imagined.

He does not stop when his head breaks the surface but
strikes out for the raft in an impatient, choppy freestyle.
He is swimming now as much to generate warmth as to
reach the raft. He kicks his legs so that his whole body is
moving in the freezing water. His scalp aches and his ears
are immediately sore but he keeps swimming out. All he
can hear is the muted sound of his own breathing and the
loud splash and slosh as he pulls in to his stroke. To forget
the pain he lets his mind wander.

'Not here.'

Bill was suddenly standing in front of Andrew. 'Son.
We have to talk.'

His father's voice sounded hoarse as though he had
a heavy cold. He was wearing the navy-blue suit Andrew

remembered from weddings and other funerals. His tie was lopsided where the knot bulged at his throat. Tonia had been over with her family by the tea and coffee, near the door to the chapel. Everyone had drifted into two groups — his and hers.

No, three groups. And his father. Bill was apart from everyone.

People stood around saying how beautiful the funeral was. The kids from Liam's kindergarten had trooped up one by one and put flowers on the casket and some of them had painted pictures for Liam. GOODBYE LIAM they said in bright paint with smeared letters. The picture that had struck Andrew most showed Liam being eaten by a bright red dragon. When you think about it, Death is like that — the red dragon that comes and eats you up.

As his father stood waiting in front of him, Andrew became aware of snippets of conversations people were having close by. Tonia's cousin admired the flowers. (There were flowers everywhere, here and at the house — he felt as though he were being smothered by flowers.) Another woman murmured that the priest had done a wonderful job. Someone else muttered darkly that the sausage rolls were only lukewarm. But all the time he could tell that everyone was really watching him. Son and father standing facing each other. *The* father and his son. What can they say to each other, poor things.

That was the first time they had faced off since Liam had died. Bill had spent the three days organising. Taking matters in hand. When everyone else was bawling their eyes out, Bill was ringing funeral directors, booking the church, ensuring that the notice in the paper was in on time. At one point Andrew had leaned against the wall in

the hallway at his parents' home and listened to Bill talking
to the caterers about whether they actually needed sausage
rolls. Andrew had listened, incredulous, as his father
haggled over the price. He insisted he would only pay
forty-five cents each.

'That was his way of coping,' Tonia had said later. He
shook his head and they had had a fight. The first of many.

And now his father was standing in front of him
outside the chapel. It had been four days exactly since
Andrew had dropped Liam off for an afternoon with his
grandparents. It had been twenty minutes since he had
helped load his son's perversely small coffin on to the silent
rollers in the back of the hearse.

'Andrew . . .' Bill said, beginning again.

'I can't talk to you. I don't want to ever talk to you
again.' Andrew had simply turned and walked away and
out the door.

He is lying on his back on the raft in the sun and he thinks
that he may have been asleep. The hammering has stopped.
He rolls over on to his side and looks toward the bach.

His father is standing on the rocky shore. He is looking
in the direction of the raft, although Andrew cannot tell
if Bill is looking at him or beyond to the far side of the lake
and the bush. Bill is wearing his old yellow togs and
Andrew can clearly see the long pale scar from the bypass.
His father raises his hand but Andrew does not wave back.

He watches as Bill wades into the lake and begins to
swim out. His father is a slow, methodical swimmer. He
keeps his head slightly too high, breathing forward rather
than to the side as children are taught. His feet kick only
occasionally, chopping up the dark water behind him.

The sun is hot on Andrew's shoulders but his skin still feels shrunken and tight from the cold water. The gaps in the wooden boards have pressed into his back. He stands and watches Bill swimming towards him. Can't he leave well enough alone? What is there left to talk about? Andrew considers diving in and swimming to shore before Bill arrives. What will they talk about when he gets here? Liam? The accident? Where to go from here? Probably not. Bill is a practical man, good with his hands; and he is Bill's son. He knows that neither of them has the vocabulary for grief.

Bill is about halfway to the raft when Andrew sees him stop mid-stroke. As though he has run into something hidden just below the surface. He begins to tread water awkwardly and Andrew sees the look of pain on his face as he reaches down. It could be cramp. Or his heart again. Bill's head goes under and then comes back up. Bill looks towards him, and Andrew waits for him to call for help but he doesn't. Instead his father tries to turn and pull himself back towards the shore. He can't swim properly and goes under again.

'Bill!'

He dives flat and long from the raft and swims towards Bill with frantic strokes. He tastes the bitter-tea lake in his mouth as he lunges through the water, unsure of how far he must swim, desperate. When he finally stops, breathing hard, scanning the surface, Bill is gone. All around him the water is clear and smooth and reflects the sunlight in sequins.

'Bill! Bill!'

It is difficult to tell how far he has come. He thinks he is roughly at the spot where Bill was when he last saw him but it is impossible to say for sure.

Duck-diving down, opening his eyes in the green-black light. He cannot see far, and swims down, kicking and pulling further and deeper until his ears flare with a sharp pain and he has to hold his nose and blow hard. He pulls himself down against the buoyancy of the air in his lungs. It is dark now but he can see the bottom. Silt, fine and who knows how deep, stirs like dust as he passes close over it. He swims until he comes to a waterlogged tangle of logs and branches which rises up like a house rattled into pieces by an earthquake. He cannot see Bill. Black shadows and green light. Bubbles cling to the hairs along his arms. He searches for his father through the alien twilight with a ringing in his ears.

The phone in the hall was ringing.

'Hello.' He could hear nothing at first. No. There was a choking sound as though someone was trying to speak through a crushed windpipe. 'Hello? Who is this?'

'Andy.'

It took him a couple of seconds to realise that it was his father.

'Dad. What's the matter?' His mind had jumped ahead, imagining Liam falling, hitting his head, cutting his foot on broken glass. A visit to the emergency room, bandages, stitches. 'Dad?'

'Something's happened.'

'Where's Liam? Dad? Is he okay?'

He could hear Tonia in the shower. They had used the Sunday afternoon alone to do the shopping, to go to a café for a half-guilty coffee. They had made love slowly in the spare room in the sunlight. They had talked about the what-if of another child.

'Dad, are you there? What's happened?'

Tonia had heard the ragged edge to his words. She came into the hallway, wrapping a towel around her, and stood, long dark hair dripping on to her shoulders, watching him quizzically.

His father was speaking again. 'I was doing some work in the garage — building a birdhouse for your mother's birthday. I wasn't watching. It was only a few minutes.' Each word is an effort.

Cold had lapped over him then. Tonia was looking at him, her face framed by her dark wet hair, looking for clues on his face.

'Tell me, Dad.'

'I found him in the neighbour's pool. You've got to come, Andy.' He was sobbing now. 'Liam's drowned.'

Andrew sees his father after his own air has run out. Bill is a foetus floating among a patch of trailing weed.

He swims down, pulling desperately at the strands, using them like a lifeline. They twist around his hands, slimy and slick, but pull free from the bottom. Clouds of silt rise and hang in the water until everything is gauzed and wrapped in a grey muslin shroud.

And then Bill is right in front of him. His father's hair hangs away from his head, each strand with a will of its own. Andrew grasps him around the neck with his right arm, pulling Bill close to him so that the back of his father's head is against his chest.

His lungs are a crumpled bag, small and useless. He kicks away from the bottom and more silt rises up. Pulling with his one free arm. Kicking again. Kicking. Kicking.

He does not feel as if it is having any effect. The walls begin to draw in as he tries to swim towards the surface. He is not sure if he is rising at all. Together they are too heavy. Bill is too heavy for his one free arm. Andrew's feet kick. A burning pain in his own chest. The light leaches away and the world is getting blacker and narrower.

Out on the edge of his vision, through the black water, he can see something move in a slow glide. He can feel it watching him from among the weed, nestled in the silt with only its eyes showing. Hunting them. His one arm pulls them upward, but he knows that whatever is below will rush to drag them back before they make the surface. His vision has shrunk down so that he is moving impossibly slowly, inching along through a narrow tunnel with walls that pulsate in time with his heartbeat. So slowly that he wonders if he is moving at all. His grip on his father begins to slip. Bill is starting to slide away from him. Trying to return to the darkness below.

And then Andrew looks up and sees himself reflected in the surface of the lake.

It is an endless silver mirror. He can see his own face upturned, pale and worried. They are small, figures in the middle distance, but he can see them both and knows that he may be able to make it. He grips Bill tighter, pulls and kicks towards the vision of himself. He is using his final strength, hidden even from himself until now. The water becomes lighter and begins to change temperature. He cannot look away or he will be lost. Whatever is moving below him, shadowing them, he can still feel it. It is just waiting for him to look away, to look back, and then it will strike.

Andrew can see himself and his father edging up, larger and larger. At the last second he reaches out his hand to touch his own outstretched fingers. The mirror shatters.

He gulps and sucks in lungfuls of air, pulls his father's head above the surface and tows him, heavy, to the raft. With his last strength, Andrew drags Bill painfully on to it, scraping his own arms and his father's back red against the wood. He leans his ear close to his father's chest and hears Bill's heart beating faintly, but there is no breath. He begins to blow into him. Bill lies on his back with his arms out from his side, pale, spreadeagled on the wood, the water lapping and sloshing between the boards against the back of his head.

Andrew pushes air down into his father's lungs again and again until there is only the huffing sound of his own breath. And again. Until his own hair is dry in the sun. 'Come on. Come on. Don't you die as well, you old bastard.' Andrew is shouting now. 'Breathe! Breathe! You're just doing this because you're stubborn. Breathe! If you die I'll never forgive you. Breathe!'

Until Bill coughs and vomits black water.

'Dad.'

Bill does not open his eyes but struggles, moving his arms. Instinctively he tries to roll on to his side. Andrew helps him, and more water gushes from his father's mouth on to the planks. Bill's mouth grimaces and he says something which Andrew does not understand. A rasping sigh.

'It's okay, Dad. I've got you. You're going to be okay.' He shifts himself and lifts his father's head so that it is resting against his leg. He strokes Bill's thin hair where a lifetime of sun has left dark marks on the skin. On the shore he sees his mother and his wife return from their walk. They have seen them now and are starting to run towards the beach. He raises his free hand and waves.

As Andrew waits for the women to row the dinghy out across the lake he is aware of something below him, under the raft, something large and black, flicking away through the water, returning to the dark places beneath.

tuesday's child

In the beginning there were just the two of us but we were not happy. And then came the video tape. It arrived in our letter box wrapped in heavy white cardboard. It was,' she says, 'a Tuesday.'

This is how she always begins the story. Anne sits on her knee (or later, when she is older, at her feet on the floor) and listens, face turned upwards towards her like a dark flower.

The quality of the image is not top-notch. Whoever operates the camera is unfamiliar with the niceties of tracking or focus. A patch of wall. The foot of a metal crib with a sheet hanging down. And then a toddler, a girl of course, with black hair and a full-moon face, standing, hands behind her back, staring earnestly up. There is a woman's voice close to the microphone speaking in Mandarin. The toddler makes no response. Cut suddenly to a new scene. A white room with a low table and chair. It is the same toddler playing with some wooden blocks. There is a man with her. He is wearing a grey suit and it is impossible to see his face. He hands the child the blocks and encourages her to stack them. Later, the man passes her a plastic doll and the child holds it upside down by the leg. She turns and speaks to whoever is holding the camera in a piccolo voice. The man leads her through a number of tasks involving blocks and pieces of jigsaw. It is only near the end that the child gets agitated and swings the doll so that its head strikes the edge of the table with a plastic *thunk* which is picked up clearly by the camera's microphone. *Thunk. Thunk. Thunk.* Cut to black.

Ruth and Simon take the video to a child psychologist in Thorndon. 'We are concerned,' says Ruth and then pauses, lost. She has so many concerns that she is uncertain which one to mention first.

'Particularly about the doll,' picks up Simon. 'She seems . . . aggressive towards it.'

Doctor Rosanowski consults his notes. 'It's impossible to get a full picture just from a video but I can tell you that there don't appear to be any *obvious* developmental problems. She's doing all the usual things you'd expect at twenty-two months. Her mobility seems good. Her fine motor skills are normal.'

'But her emotional development?' asks Ruth.

'It's very hard to tell. Although this particular orphanage is reputedly one of the better ones, they are most likely understaffed and under-resourced. Experience shows that the children grow up without building significant attachments to any specific adults. This, obviously, creates problems.'

Ruth squeezes her hands together tightly in her lap. 'But in this case can you see evidence of any major problems?'

'No. There's no evidence of that on the tape. But, as I said, it's impossible to tell from a five-minute video. The truth is that in a situation like this it's a bit of a lottery.'

Simon has chosen the fish over the beef and is hard at work with the plastic knife and fork. Ruth's meal hovers in front of her untouched. She is thinking about what Dr Rosanowski said about a lottery. Will they be lucky or unlucky with their choice?

They have decided to call the girl Isabella. It is the name she picked out when they still imagined that they could have children naturally (Isabella for a girl, Duncan for a boy). Focusing on this name has been a comfort to her over the last few months while the torturous adoption arrangements were being put in place. She said it to herself a hundred times a day: silently and out loud; while showering; waiting at the traffic lights; sitting at her desk; last thing at night. 'Is-a-bell-a.' Those four mouth-opening syllables have been something to hold on to and caress.

But somewhere over the vast Pacific, dread has seeped into her. Ruth's excitement is eroded, washed away like an unstable hillside by streams below the surface. She can feel doubt shifting the material on which she has built her future.

Mister Chen from the Celestial Stairway Adoption Agency fails to meet them at Beijing Airport as arranged. They collect their luggage and wait on plastic seats for almost two hours, then decide to catch a taxi to their hotel. Ruth asks at reception but there is no message.

'We'll just stay close to our room,' says Simon. 'He's

bound to call soon.'

Ruth looks around the hotel's vast foyer with its central fountain cascading water into a blue-tiled pond. A toddler leans out dangerously over the pond and is snatched back by its mother. Simon is still talking, although it is hard to tell if he is talking to her. 'If worst comes to worst we can phone the agency at home. They can sort it out.'

People bustle around her and she feels alone and alien. She has no business being here. The whole idea is a terrible mistake.

'Love? Are you okay? You look pale.'

'I'm fine. You're right, we can always call.'

Their room is on the twenty-seventh floor. Through the haze the city stretches out ahead of her. There are cranes everywhere, lanky, long necked, yanking up more and more buildings through the holes they have poked in the polluted air. These were not the cranes she had imagined when she thought of her new daughter's homeland.

Mr Chen shows up at 6.30 the next morning. He is not what she expected either. He is younger for a start, only about twenty-one or -two. Ruth blinks out at him from the doorway of their darkened room. Mr Chen is wearing a Hawaiian shirt under a black leather jacket.

'Who is it?' asks Simon from the bed. 'Mr Chen?'

He smiles, showing a set of teeth so large and white that they can only be dentures. 'Okay. You come now. Bus waiting.' There is no apology for not showing up at the airport. 'Bus waiting,' he says again more urgently, and he looks down the corridor as though the bus is right there idling next to the lift.

There is no time for a shower. Simon and Ruth whisper

to each other as they dress, throw some essentials into a day-bag and five minutes later find themselves following Mr Chen like dishevelled refugees being led to safety through the hotel lobby and out into the Beijing dawn.

They are not alone on the minibus. There are two other couples. Directly across the aisle sit a husband and wife who, it transpires, are from Birmingham: a round-faced man with several chins and his equally sprawling spouse. There is also an Italian couple who sit directly behind the driver, dressed head to toe in suave black, aloof as circus acrobats.

In contrast, the Birmingham couple do not stop talking. Ruth and Simon listen as they tell the story of years of trying, failed IVF treatment and impossibly long waiting lists to adopt back home.

'I wonder how long it will take to get there,' says Ruth, looking out the window at a scene of snarled traffic that for ten minutes has been as unchanging as a painting. She can feel the dread start to flow through her again, silent below the surface. What are they doing here?

Mr Chen stands at the front, snapping instructions at the driver and pointing out gaps in the traffic only he can see. His perfectly white teeth flash in the early morning light. The Birmingham woman looks across at Ruth. 'They told us the orphanage was well out of the city. Could take bleedin' hours. Not to worry though. It'll give us a chance to get to know each other.'

In the end they are on the minibus for just over five hours, not counting two short toilet stops. It takes three hours to negotiate their way out of Beijing and another two driving though barren fields and small satellite towns before they arrive. At the orphanage Ruth disembarks with stiff legs and thinks of deep vein thrombosis and the irony of falling over dead from a roaming blood clot just as they arrive. She wonders if, technically, you can orphan an orphan. Not that Isabella has been formally adopted. Ruth is reassured by the thought that they still have the chance to pull out if they do not like what they see today.

There are no children playing behind the tall mesh fence. The orphanage is simply a large brick building, like a factory, set next to a wide and dirty-looking river. In fact it might originally have been built as a factory. The road running past leads to a utilitarian bridge, and cars and trucks move by in an almost constant stream.

'We here. You come now. Hurry.' Mr Chen herds them inside where they are met by a small smiling man in a neat grey suit who they are told is the director of the orphanage. The Italians hang back by the door as Mr Chen translates the director's lengthy welcome. Ruth listens for the shouts of children but hears only the barking of a nearby dog and the hum of cars going over the bridge.

'Come,' translates Mr Chen at last. 'I show you the children.'

The three couples are ushered into a room where three small girls are standing in a strict line facing the door. Ruth recognises Isabella immediately. She is the smallest of the three and is wearing the same yellow dress as in the video. Instead of feeling the wave of joy and maternal love that she had long anticipated, Ruth feels the dread surge and swell inside her. How is it possible that they are preparing to take this child, this miniature stranger, home with them? The idea is ridiculous.

The director makes another, only slightly shorter speech and then all three couples move forward, isolating their assigned child from the small herd and shepherding her off to a far corner of the room.

Now that they are together the girl does not look to Ruth like an Isabella. It sounds silly but she is somehow more . . . *Asian* than the video led them to believe. But it is more than that. There is a watchfulness, a stillness that is at odds with the jaunty Romance name. Isabellas dance with their arms in the air. Isabellas laugh with abandon. Ruth cannot visualise this child doing either. The girl stares at the floor, and Ruth watches as the name Isabella evaporates syllable by syllable up into the orphanage air.

'What,' she says, 'was the name they gave her here?'

She has been told but cannot now remember the singsong Chinese sounds and so for the moment the child appears to her to be adrift between names like someone who is dangerously swimming from one island to the next.

'I've forgotten,' says Simon.

Of course the girl speaks no English. Ruth has learnt to say her own name in Mandarin by befriending someone from the office whose parents were Chinese immigrants. 'My name is Ruth. His name is Simon. It is very nice to meet you.'

The child stares at her blankly.

'Your accent,' says Mr Chen from where he is loitering by the wall, a blank look on his face. 'You speak Chinese very bad.'

At a dead end, Ruth looks to Simon for the lead. He holds out the wrapped parcel they've carried with them in their hand luggage from New Zealand.

The child stares at it impassively. 'Perhaps *we* should

unwrap it,' says Ruth. It is a large Pooh Bear, yellow and red. Simon holds it up, jiggling it in front of the child's face.

'Hello, little girl,' he says in a bear's deep voice. 'My name is Poooooh. What's your name?'

The child stares bug eyed, then lets out a primitive howl and begins to cry uncontrollably.

Up close the river is surprisingly wide. The banks have been fortified with steeply sloping walls of concrete. 'Probably,' suggests Simon, 'to protect against flooding.' Below them the water is a yellow-brown and seems quite high and fast. Ruth watches the currents swirl in circles.

They have been with the girl several hours but have made no tangible progress. Although they have not made her cry again, she is as impassive and disinterested as a puppet, hardly speaking, never smiling. At last Ruth suggested to Simon that they take a break, and the two of them have walked to the river, leaving the English and Italian couples who seem to be having more success.

A child was what she always wanted, but *this* child? So stern. So passive. So different from everything she had imagined. Ruth thinks about what type of things an orphan could have been exposed to in twenty-three months of life: shocking things, terrible things that don't bear thinking about.

Simon throws a large stone out into the river. 'What are you thinking?'

'That it's not too late to change our minds.'

'But we've come all this way.'

'We could just think of it as a holiday.'

'Are you serious?'

Ruth is not sure if she *is* serious. Is her doubt only an

attack of cold feet? She remembers how she felt before her wedding — as uncertain and edgy as a lone ewe. She looks down into the flowing water and folds her arms over her chest to protect against the cold wind that has sprung up. No, it is more fundamental than an attack of nerves. They *are* making a mistake.

She is about to say as much to Simon when there is a shout. A woman is coming along the bank towards them. She is carrying a bundle of sticks under one arm and she gestures and waves with her free hand, calling out again.

When she arrives in front of them, Ruth sees that the woman is about her own age and dressed against the cold in several tatty layers. Her long hair is tied back. She babbles in Mandarin and gestures towards the river and then back towards the orphanage. 'I'm sorry,' says Ruth, smiling too broadly. 'We don't understand.'

The woman places one dirty hand just above Ruth's elbow and tries to pull her away with surprising strength. Simon steps forward protectively. 'Hang on. No. No. Don't do that.' Undeterred, the woman lets go but keeps talking loudly and pointing towards the river. Ruth wishes she had taken the time to learn more useful phrases.

'Keep walking,' suggests Simon. 'She's probably trying to sell us something. Just walk away.'

They walk back along the bank towards the orphanage but the woman follows them. She grows increasingly agitated. Her voice rises into an almost-shout. She tugs at their clothes.

Ruth is starting to feel afraid when Mr Chen appears beside them, the collar of his Hawaiian shirt flapping in the wind. He speaks loudly to the woman, waving his leather arms to shoo her away. The woman does not retreat but chatters back, pointing at the river.

'She say that you should not be here.'

'Why not?' asks Ruth.

'She say that river is dangerous.' The woman speaks again. 'That many people come here and drown. They fall down. Here. Cannot climb up again. River take them forever.'

The woman is smiling now and nodding as though she understands every word Mr Chen is saying. Ruth looks towards the concrete bank which she now realises is steeper than she first thought and covered near the bottom in a thick green sludge. The yellow water swirls past. She shudders, imagining trying to scramble up again and again, clothes heavy with water.

'Please thank her very much. It was kind of her to try and warn us.'

Mr Chen and the woman talk. 'She want to know why you here. I tell her you come from New Zealand to adopt baby girl.'

'And what did she say?' asks Ruth.

'That you very good people and that little girl is very lucky.'

In the minibus on the way back to the hotel, Ruth sits and stares out the window. It is dark outside and she can see only what is lit: the fleeting interior of a house through a half-open door; a young boy leaning against a vending machine; a group of old men standing smoking on a street corner — snippets of lives until then unimagined. Simon has fallen asleep next to her, his head back.

Next to the river they had thanked the woman again and walked away a short distance before Ruth stopped and turned back.

'Wait. Please ask her what her name is.'

Mr Chen translated and the woman replied with sounds from which Ruth had heard clearly the name Anne.

'That is what we will call her,' she thinks, and lowers her hand to place it lightly on the head of the small girl who, exhausted and confused, sleeps between them.

This is the story she tells Anne.

It has grown over the years in the retelling until it has achieved a shape like litany. Ruth is waiting for the day, which cannot be far off, when Anne will ask if the woman at the river was her real mother. Was she living close by, waiting to see if nice people would adopt her daughter into a better life?

Ruth knows that this interpretation is improbable. But who is she to deny her earnest dark flower this tantalising glimpse of a birth mother?

When the question eventually comes it is a Tuesday.

experiments in space and time

0726

He sits behind the wheel of the bus, waiting for the precise moment when he will begin. He is tall, full of angles, and appears to be folded up behind the wheel like a mathematician's half-open compass. The route starts at the top of Newton Road next to the lamppost with the green tag that could be a word or a badly drawn apple or it could be nothing. He clears his mind and focuses on the details of the first part of the journey. He knows that beginnings are crucial. He goes over it all in his mind, letting the possibilities and variables wash over him. He feels positive. He feels that things are falling into place. It has been a cold night and there is a slight frost which will not have melted by the time he begins. Even the delaying effect of the frost is included in his calculations.

0728

The bus driver's name is Morrison. It is printed on a
laminated card that also contains a photograph of himself
taken in another time, another place. The card hangs from
the sun visor so that Morrison is simultaneously driving
and looking back down the aisle of the bus, making sure
that everything is where it should be, and when. In both
his past and present Morrison wears a blue uniform with
a clean white shirt. He waits. And then, reaching out his
right hand, turns the key in the ignition. The engine turns
over, loud in the quiet suburban street. It is well tuned
and soon settles down into an easy rhythm. It is still dark
and there is an overhead light that he reaches up to and
switches off. He feels the vibrations up through his feet
and through the seat. The bus hums.

0729

It is time. His feet shift. He begins. The bus rolls forward
down the slight incline, the front bumper passing the chipped
gate of number 23. Morrison glances down, checking the
time: 37 seconds. The sun is just beginning to climb out of
the Pacific when he comes to the first roundabout on the
corner of Rowland and Rutherford. He accelerates through
it, aware that he is slightly behind. He pulls up at the stop
two-thirds of the way down Heisenberg where a man in a
dark suit is waiting with an air of uncertainty. The man
folds his paper and steps on to the bus. If he thought about
Morrison at all, the man would probably say that he likes
the driver, appreciates his punctuality and the whiteness of
his shirt. The man has a concession card which Morrison

clips. The bus rolls forward, still 8 seconds behind schedule.

0733.31

He has fastened a sleek digital clock on to the dashboard next to the speedometer. It has red numbers that flash into existence. The clock not only shows the hours and the seconds but also delves into the spaces between; the thousandths of seconds flow by like running water. To Morrison the digits appear with the brilliance of sunspots. His passengers on this day will not know it, but Morrison is carrying out the most taxing of temporal experiments. His calculations are as precise as those done by any physicist in any of the leading laboratories around the world. As the bus goes past the third post of the picket fence on J. J. Thompson Road, Morrison checks his time again. Each red number tells Morrison when the bus is in time. This is fundamental. If he is not driving, he spends hours studying the clock. He has meditated on the numbers until their changes have become instinctual to him. From his uncompromising knowledge of time, Morrison can calculate where precisely the bus should be in space.

Time and Space. They are everything to the bus driver.

0737.46

The corner of Loomis, turning left into Schrodinger. He is slightly ahead of where he should be now: as much as 3 seconds. The absence of passengers at the last two stops has thrown his calculations out. Morrison eases off the accelerator as a cat crosses the road ahead of him and the bus glides, shedding seconds like a skin as it slips through the air. The barren robinia with the split branch goes past. Morrison notes its passing, using the straight inside edge of his wing mirror as his point of reference. Just as he has an intimate knowledge of the smallest units of time, Morrison must know the geography of his route. Of course he knows every bus stop but beyond that he is familiar with the lampposts, houses, fences, hedges, trees, roundabouts and letter boxes — everything that he must pass. And not just as it is seen from the bus. He walks the route regularly. He believes that it is important to change his perspective in order to gain a more thorough insight into his terrain. Often, in the evening, he can be seen moving briskly along the footpaths. In his hands he carries a measuring tape and a builders' level. Occasionally he stops to inspect a newly painted letter box or to confirm the distance between two points. Everything is a measuring stick for the bus's passing.

0742.22

The near edge of the driveway of the house with the yellow garden gnome . . .

0746.16

The corner of Gouldsmit Crescent . . .

0753.29

The cracked glass door of the Indian dairy . . .

0801.53

The mark like a swelling cloud where white paint once spilled from the back of a van in the middle of Oppenheimer Street . . .

0802.48

He is doing well today but it is a struggle. Achieving the exact now and when for brief periods is not enough. Morrison aims to maintain. That is his ultimate goal. He must calculate precisely what changes, minute adjustments to speed and location, he must make to ensure that his bus continues to be where and when it should be. The calculations in his head are constantly changing. The numbers alter, slipping by like tyres on a greasy surface. The foibles of traffic flow are his constant nemesis. He must factor in the long queues of people on rainy days, the reduced speed that greasy roads demand, the pushchairs that must be fastened to the front of the bus, road works, jaywalkers, accidents. Once a large dog was struck by a car immediately in front of him and lay, dying slowly, in the middle of the road for 2 minutes and 13 seconds before it finally expired and was dragged aside.

0803.23

As he begins to cross the Bohr Street bridge, Morrison feels a subtle change. There is a tingle up along the hairs of his lower back as he looks down at his clock and sees that he is within a second, less than a second, of where he should be, and has been for 23 continuous seconds now.

There are so many variables. He feels the sweat begin to trickle down the side of his face. He is so close. Despite the tension, his mind feels clear. His thoughts rush ahead, sweeping away the impediments from his route. This is why he sits alone at night in his house surrounded by his maps and his books and his instruments for measuring time and space. He lives alone. The rigours such experimentation demands are not possible for a family man. Every evening he spreads his tools out in front of him on the large battered desk. Detailed city maps with notes in his economical hand down the margin; aerial photographs; the latest calculator in a plastic cover; pages covered in mathematical formulae. His shelves are filled with books about the nature of time and space. Morrison has an ongoing correspondence with a professor of The Philosophy of Science at Boston University who believes that Morrison is perpetuating some standing joke when he insists that he is a bus driver. The professor tells his colleagues that Morrison must be, at the very least, a gifted postgraduate. When pressed for details about the exact nature of his work, all that Morrison will say is that he is conducting an important experiment.

0805.121

He has almost succeeded. Morrison's mind itself begins to accelerate. The variables crowd his head. He can see endless possibilities stretching out in front of him like a landscape. Countless corrections come to him so that he can keep to his schedule. His foot eases down on the accelerator, fingers barely gripping the wheel. The bus seems to be flying. Morrison is intimately acquainted with every *where* on the road and passes each point at an exact *when*. He takes the sharp corners as though the bus were on rails. He slips it through impossible spaces. The bus swings from side to side, but his passengers do not seem to notice. They trust the driver as he accelerates away with one eye on the glowing red numbers which, in his mind, seem to fill the whole windscreen.

0806.0931

It happens at the bridge over the river at the intersection of Michelson and Einstein. Morrison's bus has never been so *here*, so *now* for so long. In his mind Morrison has begun to factor in the extra thrust of the faint easterly breeze down the straight, the restraining hand of the air as it eddies between the city buildings, the friction as late-autumn leaves catch beneath the wheels. The flap of a butterfly's wing in central China. Only in his imagination have time and space ever meshed so precisely. Traffic is light and seems to melt in front of him. The bus flashes past the old courthouse, past shop doors, knots in the trunks of trees, the faded edge of a circus poster on a brick wall, a crack in the footpath, at exactly the right moment. The right second. The right thousandth of a second. Much smaller units of time. Numbers slot into place. Morrison feels it, feels as if even his blood has begun to move to its own precise schedule.

0807.133567

None of his passengers notice as the bus attains perfection.

my father running with a dead boy

At my father's funeral an old man in a crumpled black suit gets up to speak. He rises slowly on old man's legs from among the dark suits and neatly combed heads, murmuring apologies for flattened toes and kicked handbags. For a moment I think that he is my father. The same old man's shuffling walk. But then I see that, no, they are different people. This man's nose is larger, more Roman.

It's a good turn-out. Better than I would have thought for a man as quiet and solitary as my father. I close my eyes and see him coming towards me, walking as he always did, stiffly, head down, shoulders hunched as though moving into a strong wind. By the time I was ten my father was already an old man, slow and careful in his movements. No cricket on the back lawn or kicks with the rugby ball down at the park.

I dread the awkward silence which always hovers near us. Soon I will begin to talk about the rugby or the latest rates increase, although I don't really care about either, and then, inevitably, hating the cliché, I will work my way around to the rainy spell we've had lately. What does he think, will it be a hard winter?

I open my eyes and my father vanishes.

Someone has forgotten to turn the heating on. The church is a meat-locker, despite the sunlight coming through the stained-glass window behind the coffin. I stare at the colours on the pale carpet where the filtered light spreads like spilt fizzy drink — Fanta, Mello Yello, Raspberry, Lemon-Lime.

Several people have already spoken. My father's boss from the insurance office said a few words. He took a piece of paper from his pocket, smoothed it with fat sweaty fingers and, head down, mumbled into the microphone. From the front row I stared at his waist where the black suit bulged out over his belt.

'A sad day for family and friends sorely missed a diligent worker cared about his job in thirty years never a complaint punctual a good provider a great loss our condolences to Helen and Greg.'

The old man in the crumpled suit moves across in front of me. He wades into the pool of spilt drink which splashes up over his black shoes and halfway up his legs, and taps the microphone with a thin finger. I see that there are dark spots on the backs of his hands. Surprisingly, he seems to change his mind about the microphone and steps around in front of it.

'I hope you can hear me. Never liked these things much.' His voice is deeper and stronger than I had expected. It's an actor's voice or someone who's used to telling a good yarn. A younger man's voice.

Out of the corner of my eye I think I see my father shuffling forward to listen, shoulders stooped. But when I turn my head there is nothing. A thick drape stirred by a draught in a shadowy corner.

'I don't expect many of you know me. My name's Reginald Black, but Ray used to call me Blacky and after that most other people did too. I was Ray's best mate right though from when we were about sixteen to when I moved up to Napier. That was when I was twenty-five. A fair few years ago now. We used to play rugby together on a Saturday for Brighton and we'd go to the local afterwards for a few beers. On a Friday night we'd drive to the dances in town, hoping to meet a couple of girls who wouldn't mind going for a ride in Ray's car after it was all over. Most weeks we'd find a couple who were game.'

And then, amazingly, he winks, a slow old man's wink and he's looking right at me when he does it. A few people laugh nervously, unsure if this type of talk is suitable for a funeral. The old man's skin is very brown and I have a sudden image of him down on his knees, digging in rich black soil, a tomato plant in his dirt-caked hand.

Out of the corner of my eye I notice my father shuffle forward again. I don't turn to look this time, and he remains there in the corner listening.

'But what I mostly remember about Ray is the time he carried the dead boy home.' I look up, not sure if I have heard the old man correctly. 'We were both still living with our parents at the time. We must have been twenty or so. We lived down by the beach and Ray was building a small sailboat in the shed out the back. Nothing fancy. Just something to potter around in on weekends, and sometimes I'd go over and give him a hand. We'd take the frame out and put it on a couple of saw-horses. It was good working outside like that. Ray's parents' house backed on to a reserve down by the estuary. Big pine trees kept the wind off and we could hear the surf as we worked if the wind was right.

'This particular day, I remember it was hot and Ray wasn't wearing a shirt. He was brown and covered in sweat and sawdust from the work. As we sanded down the hull we'd seen a couple of kids playing in the reserve, running in and out of the trees, shouting and laughing, playing cops and robbers or such like. One of them was Trevor O'Brien. His mother lived two doors down from Ray. They had a dog with them.

'Then after a while we heard the dog barking. The barking went on and on, and not like when the kids were playing near us either. The dog was pretty good then. It was a strange barking, all high and excited like it had treed a possum or maybe got itself tangled up in a fence. After a bit of that, Ray and me looked at each other, and I remember Ray said something like, "Let's go and have a look, eh?"

'It was cold in the shade of the pines after being in the sun. There was no undergrowth, just a thick mat of brown pine needles on the ground. We walked at first, a good excuse for a break, but as the dog's barks got louder Ray started running. I don't know why, I never asked. He just started running. Ray went up a trail between the lupins and I lost sight of him in the sand hills. I followed, and came to a clearing with walls of sand all around. Not the sloping, dry white sand that you get down by the water but a harder mixture of sand and earth and clay that made steeper walls. It had been raining a bit that week and the sand was wet and dark. All around the top lupins blocked out the sun. It was like being in a pit. The dog was over in one corner, whimpering and digging in the sand.

'By the time I arrived Ray was down on his knees with his back to me and he was digging too. 'What's happening? What's going on?' You see, even then I still didn't understand. But when I got close enough to see properly I understood all right. Sticking out of the sand was a kid's foot and part of his leg. Trevor O'Brien and his cobber had got bored with cops and robbers so they'd dug a tunnel into the hard sand wall. They'd dug a pretty good tunnel too, big enough for them to both crawl inside. There was a good-sized pile of sand next to where Ray was kneeling, so I reckoned they'd dug back a fair ways. A great little tunnel. Until it collapsed in on top of them.

'Ray grabbed the kid's leg and pulled. He was a big bloke, big broad shoulders and back. With Ray pulling, that kid came out of the sand like a cork coming out of a bottle. It was Trevor's friend. Ray never even looked at him. He just handed him to me like a sack of potatoes. "Get him to my place. Get a doctor." And then he was down on his knees again, digging.

'A ten-year-old kid weighs a fair bit but I ran with him bouncing up and down on my shoulder all the way to the house. Ray's mum had been a nurse during the war and she knew what to do, although she got a hell of a surprise when I crashed through her kitchen door. I watched, sucking down air in great gulps, as she cleared the sand out of the kid's mouth and blew into him. He was lying on the kitchen table. I watched his chest rise up with every blow that Ray's mum put into him. When the doctor finally arrived the kid was coughing up sand, but I didn't wait to see what happened. I ran back through the trees to Ray.

'He was still digging. He'd had the idea of digging down from above on more of an angle. The sand was wetter higher up from the rain and didn't cave in so easy, plus the roots of the lupins held it together more. He'd dug enough so that only his legs from the knees down still showed. I hollered at him that I was there and he yelled back for me to help move the sand piling up in the entrance to his tunnel. He was pushing it back between his legs and I grabbed the sand and flung it away until my shoulders ached, but no matter how much sand I moved Ray always pushed out more. After a while not even his feet showed and I had to lean right into the tunnel to scoop out the sand. All the time the dog sat and watched and whined.

'A long time after, I heard Ray shout something I didn't understand and he pushed out more sand and then he began backing out of the hole. I grabbed his legs and pulled. Ray was dragging the kid by the shoulders, but as soon as I saw him I knew that Trevor was dead. Mostly from his eyes. They were half open and the eyeballs were covered in sand and some ran out from his nose and the corners of his mouth.

'Ray was gasping from the digging but he held the dead boy in front of him like a baby and began to run. I ran along behind, but even with the kid Ray was faster than me. He fair flew between the trees. I remember that his feet flicked up dry pine needles as he passed. The dog ran behind barking.'

The old man pauses and looks out over the people. Out of the corner of my eye my father moves again, shuffling away. He's heard enough.

'I was right. Trevor O'Brien was dead. As near as I can figure it, he was under the sand for half an hour. We went to the funeral. Mrs O'Brien's husband had died of a heart attack a few years before and she only had the one child, so she took it badly. Ray took it pretty hard too — that he hadn't saved them both.

'Well, I reckon that's all I want to say. After I moved to Napier we lost touch. Neither of us were great letter writers. But Ray was a good mate, a good person. For years after, he'd visit Mrs O'Brien, help out with repairs around the house and gardening and such. And you know, when he was digging that tunnel, all I could think of was that it was going to cave in like the other one and then Ray would be dead too. But when I asked him about it after, he said he hadn't even thought about that. He was just thinking about the boy.'

The old man steps off the carpet and begins the long walk up the aisle. His walking stick clicks and clatters on the stone floor. As he passes me, he turns his head and nods. His eyes are the same shade of blue as my father's.

After the echo of the final hymn has faded from the rafters I help to carry my father's coffin up the aisle. It slides easily into the waiting hearse.

A small river runs by the church, and as we wait for someone to bring around the car I walk away over the lawn and down to the water. Looking across to the opposite bank I see a young man with blond wavy hair standing under a tree. He is not wearing a shirt, and the reflection of the light off the water plays over his tanned body. He is sweating, and damp sand clings to his skin in patches.

In his arms he holds a dead boy. He cradles him gently as though the boy weighs nothing, a baby. The young man looks at me for a long moment and then smiles gently, happy to be alive and young. Turning, he begins to run. He runs along the river bank, smooth and easy despite the boy in his arms. His feet kick up dry pine needles as he passes.

I watch until my father disappears between the tall trunks of the pine trees.

acknowledgements

'King Tut's Last Feather' was broadcast by Radio New Zealand, 2000.

'The Apple of His Eye' first appeared in *Sport*, Vol 24, Summer 2000, edited by James Brown and Catherine Chidgey; and was broadcast by Radio New Zealand, 2000.

'The Battle of Crete' was broadcast by Radio New Zealand, 2003.

'The Seduction' was broadcast by Radio New Zealand, 2005.

'Like Wallpaper' first appeared in the anthology *Boys' Own Stories*, edited by Graeme Lay, Tandem Press, 2000; was broadcast by Radio New Zealand, 2000; and was the title story of *Like Wallpaper: New Zealand Short Stories for Teenagers*, edited by Barbara Else, Random House, 2005.

'Dreams of a Suburban Mercenary' was broadcast by Radio New Zealand, 2002.

'Fish 'n' Chip Shop Song' was purchased by Radio New Zealand, 2002.

'Weight' was first published in the *Sunday Star-Times*, 1999; and broadcast by Radio New Zealand, 2000.

'The Raft' was purchased by Radio New Zealand in 2003; and first published in the *Timaru Herald*, 2004.

'Tuesday's Child' was broadcast by Radio New Zealand, 2005.

'Experiments in SPACE and TIME' was first published in the *Christchurch Press*, 2003; and broadcast by Radio New Zealand, 2004.

'My Father Running with a Dead Boy' was first published in the *Sunday Star-Times*, 1997; broadcast by Radio New Zealand, 1999; appeared in *Authors' Choice*, edited by Owen Marshall, Penguin, 2001; and in *Essential New Zealand Short Stories*, edited by Owen Marshall, Random House, 2002.